WHEN CHU...

'Tis now the very witching time of night
When churchyards yawn and hell itself breathes out
Contagion to the world.
Hamlet, William Shakespeare

Also edited by Denys Val Baker:

Ghosts in Country Houses
Cornish Ghost Stories
Stories of the Supernatural
Stories of the Occult
Stories of the Macabre
Stories of the Night
Stories of Horror and Suspense

WHEN CHURCHYARDS YAWN

An anthology of ghostly and supernatural tales

Edited by
DENYS VAL BAKER

WILLIAM KIMBER · LONDON

This collection first published in 1982 by
WILLIAM KIMBER & CO. LIMITED
Godolphin House, 22a Queen Anne's Gate,
London SW1H 9AE

ISBN 0-7183-0039 4

© by Estate of M.R. James, 1982   Fay Weldon, 1981
Ronald Duncan, 1971   Daphne du Maurier, 1980
Fred Urquhart 1980   Estate of James Turner, 1975
Frank Baker, 1982   R. Chetwynd-Hayes, 1978
Giles Gordon, 1976   Estate of Hugh Walpole 1933
Denys Val Baker, 1977   Peter Tinniswood, 1977

This book is copyright. No part of it may be reproduced in any form without permission in writing from the publishers except by a reviewer who wishes to quote brief passages in connection with a review written for inclusion in a newspaper, magazine, radio or television broadcast.

Photoset in North Wales by
Derek Doyle & Associates, Mold, Clwyd
and printed in Great Britain by
Biddles Limited, Guildford and Kings Lynn

Contents

	Editor's Introduction	7
I	Rats *M.R. James*	9
II	Spirit of the House *Fay Weldon*	16
III	When We Dead Awaken *Ronald Duncan*	29
IV	Escort *Daphne du Maurier*	33
V	Seven Ghosts in Search *Fred Urquhart*	50
VI	Act of Contrition *James Turner*	60
VII	In The Box *Frank Baker*	80
VIII	The Basket Chair *Winston Graham*	90
IX	The Sad Ghost *R. Chetwynd-Hayes*	107
X	In Spite of Himself *Giles Gordon*	126
XI	The Walking Shadow *Jean Stubbs*	137
XII	Mrs Lunt *Hugh Walpole*	151
XIII	The Anniversary *Denys Val Baker*	166
XIV	The Top Cat *Peter Tinniswood*	172

Introduction

When churchyards yawn indeed! The very image of mossy, slumbering churchyards is rather like an open invitation to some secret world, a place of swirling shadows and mysterious looming figures, a background of haunting echoes and bloodstains – where indeed at the very witching hour of night then hell itself might breathe out.

Something of this spooky atmosphere pervades many of the stories in this the latest of our series of anthologies of ghost stories, whether in the contemporary stories of such masters as Daphne du Maurier and Winston Graham or in the work of such past outstanding tellers of tales as M.R. James. At the same time variety is the spice of life (and death) and so here, too, we have an entertaining mixture of many ghostly ingredients. Jean Stubbs introduces us with much good humour to a theatrical ghost; Ronald Duncan in an extremely short cameo achieves as much impact as many stories four times as long; Frank Baker takes us to Land's End in Cornwall for the setting of his strange story; R. Chetwynd-Hayes gives us a fascinating portrait of a very sad ghost; Fred Urquhart brings on a ghost with a sense of humour; and we have lively tales from well known novelists of today: Fay Weldon, Giles Gordon and Peter Tinniswood. As for the stories contributed by Daphne du Maurier, Winston Graham and M. R. James – well, each in its own way grips the reader with practised expertise.

My thanks are due to Edward Arnold Ltd for permission to include 'Rats' by M.R. James from *The Collected Ghost Stories of M.R. James*: to the author for 'Spirit of the House' by Fay Weldon from *Watching Me Watching You* (Hodder &

Stoughton, 1981); to the author for 'When We Dead Awaken' by Ronald Duncan from *A Kettle of Fish* (W.H. Allen, 1971); to the author for 'Escort' by Daphne du Maurier from *The Rendezvous and Other Stories* (Gollancz, 1980); to the author for 'Seven Ghosts in Search' by Fred Urquhart from *Blackwood's Magazine*, 1980; to William Kimber & Co Ltd for 'Act of Contrition' by James Turner from *The Way Shadows Fall* (William Kimber 1975); to the author for 'In the Box' by Frank Baker, previously unpublished: to the author for 'The Basket Chair' by Winston Graham from *The Japanese Girl* (Collins, 1970); to the author for 'The Sad Ghost' by R. Chetwynd-Hayes from *The Fourteenth Fontana Book of Ghost Stories* (Collins, 1978); to the author for 'In Spite of Himself' by Giles Gordon from *The Ghost Book* edited by Patricia Parkin (Barrie and Jenkins, 1976); to the author for 'The Walking Shadow' by Jean Stubbs from *The Ghost Book* (Barrie and Jenkins, 1970); to Sir Rupert Hart Davis for 'Mrs Lunt' by Hugh Walpole from *All Soul's Night* (Macmillan, 1933); to William Kimber & Co Ltd for 'The Anniversary' by Denys Val Baker from *The Secret Place* (William Kimber, 1977); to the author for 'The Top Coat' by Peter Tinniswood from *The Ghost Book* edited by James Haly (Barrie & Jenkins, 1977); and to Mr G.T. Sassoon for permission to quote from Siegfried Sassoon's 'Grandeur of Ghosts'.

I

Rats

M.R. James

'And if you was to walk through the bedrooms now, you'd see the ragged, mouldy bedclothes a-heaving and a-heaving like seas.' 'And a-heaving and a-heaving with what?' he says. 'Why, with the rats under 'em.'

But was it with the rats? I ask because in another case it was not. I cannot put a date to the story, but I was young when I heard it, and the teller was old. It is an ill-proportioned tale, but that is my fault, not his.

It happened in Suffolk, near the coast. In a place where the road makes a sudden dip and then a sudden rise, as you go northward, at the top of that rise, stands a house on the left of the road. It is a tall red-brick house, narrow for its height; perhaps it was built about 1770. The top of the front is a low triangular pediment with a round window in the centre. Behind it are stables and offices, and such garden as it has is behind them. Scraggy Scotch firs are near it: an expanse of gorse-covered land stretches away from it. It commands a view of the distant sea from the upper windows of the front. A sign on a post stands before the door, or did so stand, for though it was an inn of repute once, I believe it is so no longer.

To this inn came my acquaintance, Mr Thomson, when he was a young man, on a fine spring day, coming from the University of Cambridge, and desirous of solitude in tolerable quarters, and time for reading. These he found, for the landlord and his wife had been in service and could make a visitor comfortable, and there was no one else staying in the inn. He had a large room on the first floor commanding the road and the view, and if it faced east, why, that could not be helped; the house was well built and warm.

He spent very tranquil and uneventful days: work all the morning, an afternoon perambulation of the country round, a little conversation with country company or the people of the inn in the evening over the then fashionable drink of brandy-and-water, a little more reading and writing, and bed; and he would have been content that this should continue for the full month he had at disposal, so well was his work progressing, and so fine was the April of that year – which I have reason to believe was that which Orlando Whistlecraft chronicles in his weather record as the 'charming year'.

One of his walks took him along the northern road, which stands high and traverses a wide common, called a heath. On the bright afternoon when he first chose this direction his eye caught a white object some hundreds of yards to the left of the road, and he felt it necessary to make sure what this might be. It was not long before he was standing by it, and found himself looking at a square block of white stone fashioned somewhat like the base of a pillar, with a square hole in the upper surface. Just such another you may see at this day on Thetford Heath. After taking stock of it, he contemplated for a few minutes the view, which offered a church tower or two, some red roofs of cottages, and windows winking in the sun, and the expanse of sea – also with an occasional wink and gleam upon it – and so pursued his way.

In the desultory evening talk in the bar, he asked why the white stone was there on the common.

'A' old-fashioned thing, that is,' said the landlord (Mr Betts); 'we was none of us alive when that was put there.' 'That's right,' said another. 'It stands pretty high,' said Mr Thomson, 'I dare say a sea-mark was on it some time back.' 'Ah, yes,' Mr Betts agreed, 'I 'ave 'eard they could see it from the boats; but whatever there was, it's fell to bits this long time.' 'Good job, too,' said a third; ' 'twarn't a lucky mark, by what the old men used to say; not lucky for the fishin', I mean to say.' 'Why ever not?' said Thomson. 'Well, I never see it myself,' was the answer, 'but they 'ad some funny ideas, what I mean, peculiar, them old chaps, and I shouldn't wonder but what they made away with it theirselves.'

It was impossible to get anything clearer than this: the company, never very voluble, fell silent, and when next someone spoke it was of village affairs and crops. Mr Betts was the speaker.

Not every day did Thomson consult his health by taking a country walk. One very fine afternoon found him busily writing at three o'clock. Then he stretched himself and rose, and walked out of his room into the passage. Facing him was another room, then the stair-head, then two more rooms, one looking out to the back, the other to the south. At the south end of the passage was a window, to which he went, considering with himself that it was rather a shame to waste such a fine afternoon. However, work was paramount just at the moment; he thought he would just take five minutes off and go back to it, and those five minutes he would employ – the Bettses could not possibly object – to looking at the other rooms in the passage, which he had never seen. Nobody at all, it seemed, was indoors; probably, as it was market day, they were all gone to the town, except perhaps a maid in the bar. Very still the house was, and the sun shone really hot; early flies buzzed in the window-panes. So he explored.

The room facing his own was undistinguished except for an old print of Bury St Edmunds; the two next him on his side of the passage were gay and clean, with one window apiece, whereas his had two. Remained the south-west room, opposite to the last which he had entered. This was locked; but Thomson was in a mood of quite indefensible curiosity, and, feeling confident that there could be no damaging secrets in a place so easily got at, he proceeded to fetch the key of his own room, and, when that did not answer, to collect the keys of the other three. One of them fitted, and he opened the door. The room had two windows looking south and west, so it was as bright and the sun as hot upon it as could be. Here there was no carpet, but bare boards; no pictures, no washing-stand, only a bed in the farther corner: an iron bed, with mattress and bolster, covered with a bluish check counterpane.

As featureless a room as you can well imagine, and yet there was something that made Thomson close the door very quickly and quietly behind him and lean against the window-sill in the passage, actually quivering all over. It was this: that under the counterpane someone lay, and not only lay, but stirred. That it was some*one* and not some*thing* was certain, because the shape of a head was unmistakable on the bolster; and yet it was all covered; and no one lies with covered head but a dead person; and this was not dead, not truly dead, for it heaved and shivered. If he had seen these things in dusk or by the light of a flickering candle, Thomson could have comforted himself and talked of fancy. On this bright day that was impossible.

What was to be done? First, lock the door at all costs. Very gingerly he approached it and, bending down, listened, holding his breath; perhaps there might be a sound of heavy breathing and a prosaic explanation. There was absolute silence. But as, with a rather tremulous hand, he put the key into its hole and turned it, it rattled, and on the instant a stumbling padding tread was heard coming towards the door. Thomson fled like a rabbit to his room and locked himself in: futile enough, he knew it was; would doors and locks be any obstacle to what he suspected? But it was all he could think of at the moment, and in fact nothing happened; only there was a time of acute suspense – followed by a misery of doubt as to what to do. The impulse, of course, was to slip away as soon as possible from a house which contained such an inmate.

But only the day before he had said he should be staying for at least a week more, and how, if he changed plans, could he avoid the suspicion of having pried into places where he certainly had no business? Moreover, either the Bettses knew all about the inmate, and yet did not leave the house; or knew nothing, which equally meant that there was nothing to be afraid of; or knew just enough to make them shut up the room, but not enough to weigh on their spirits: in any of these cases it seemed that not much was to be feared, and certainly so far he had had no sort of ugly experience. On the whole, the line of least resistance was to stay.

Well, he stayed out his week. Nothing took him past that

door, and, often as he would pause in a quiet hour of day or night in the passage, and listen and listen, no sound whatever issued from that direction. You might have thought that he would have made some attempt at ferreting out stories connected with the inn – hardly perhaps from Betts, but from the parson of the parish, or old people in the village; but no, the reticence which commonly falls on people who have had strange experiences, and believe in them, was upon him. Nevertheless, as the end of his stay drew near, his yearning after some kind of explanation grew more and more acute. On his solitary walks he persisted in planning out some way, the least obtrusive, of getting another daylight glimpse into that room, and eventually arrived at this scheme. He would leave by an afternoon train – about four o'clock. When his fly was waiting, and his luggage on it, he would make one last expedition upstairs to look round his own room and see if anything was left unpacked, and then, with that key, which he had contrived to oil (as if that made any difference!) the door should once more be opened for a moment, and shut.

So it worked out. The bill was paid, the consequent small talk gone through while the fly was loaded: 'Pleasant part of the country – been very comfortable, thanks to you and Mrs Betts – hope to come back some time,' on one side; on the other: 'Very glad you've found satisfaction, sir, done our best – always glad to 'ave your good word – very much favoured we've been with the weather, to be sure.' Then, 'I'll just take a look upstairs in case I've left a book or something out – no, don't trouble, I'll be back in a minute.' And as noiselessly as possible he stole to the door and opened it. The shattering of the illusion! He almost laughed aloud. Propped, or you might say sitting, on the edge of the bed was – nothing in the round world but a scarecrow! A scarecrow out of the garden, of course, dumped into the deserted room. ... Yes; but here amusement ceased. Have scarecrows bare, bony feet? Do their heads loll on to their shoulders? Have they iron collars and links of chain about their necks? Can they get up and move, if never so stiffly, across a floor, with wagging head and arms close at their sides? And shiver?

The slam of the door, the dash to the stair-head, the leap downstairs were followed by a faint. Awaking, Thomson saw Betts standing over him with the brandy-bottle and a very reproachful face. 'You shouldn't 'a' done so, sir, really you shouldn't. It ain't a kind way to act by persons as done the best they could for you.' Thomson heard words of this kind, but what he said in reply he did not know. Mr Betts, and perhaps even more Mrs Betts, found it hard to accept his apologies and his assurances that he would say no word that could damage the good name of the house. However, they *were* accepted. Since the train could not now be caught, it was arranged that Thomson should be driven to the town to sleep there.

Before he went the Bettses told him what little they knew. 'They says he was landlord 'ere a long time back, and was in with the 'ighwaymen that 'ad their beat about the 'eath. That's how he come by his end: 'ung in chains, they say, up where you see that stone what the gallus stood in. Yes, the fishermen made away with that, I believe, because they see it out at sea and it kep' the fish off, according to their idea. Yes, we 'ad the account from the people that 'ad the 'ouse before we come. "You keep that room shut up," they says, "but don't move the bed out, and you'll find there won't be no trouble." And no more there 'as been; not once he haven't come out into the 'ouse, though what he may do now there ain't no sayin'. Anyway, you're the first I know on that's seen him since we've been 'ere; I never set eyes on him myself, nor don't want. And ever since we've made the servants' rooms in the stablin', we ain't 'ad no difficulty that way. Only I do 'ope, sir, as you'll keep a close tongue, considerin' 'ow an 'ouse do get talked about'; with more to this effect.

The promise of silence was kept for many years. The occasion of my hearing the story at last was this: that when Mr Thomson came to stay with my father it fell to me to show him to his room, and instead of letting me open the door for him, he stepped forward and threw it open himself, and then for some moments stood in the doorway holding up his candle and looking narrowly into the interior. Then he seemed to recollect himself and said: 'I beg your pardon. Very absurd, but I can't help doing that, for a particular reason.' What that reason was I heard some few days afterwards and you have heard now.

II

Spirit of the House

Fay Weldon

Some time after the trouble with Jenny began, Christine wrote off to a professor of psychical research who lived in California. 'Whenever Jenny comes into the room,' Christine wrote, 'I feel cold. So I know there's *something* wrong with her. But what exactly it is?' She had an answer sooner than she expected. The professor wrote that the presence of evil was often registered, by sensitives, in this manner; and was there a bad smell as well?

Now Jenny did indeed quite often smell strongly of carbolic but Christine felt that this was not in itself significant. The soap provided for employees up at the Big House was a job-lot of hard, orange, carbolic tablets, bought cheap from an army surplus store, and Jenny washed herself with it, lavishly and often. Christine always took Mornay's Lavender to work with her, the more sweetly to wash her pretty hands. Christine liked to smell nice, and her husband Luke liked her to smell nice, and how he could put up with Jenny smelling of carbolic, Christine could not understand. And how he could love her, Christine could understand still less.

But carbolic was not, in itself, a bad smell, and nothing like the stench of sulphur and decomposition associated with the presence of the devil. Enough however, that the feeling of cold wafted around Jenny like an odour. She could be said to smell cold. Christine discontinued her correspondence with the Californian professor for fear of discovering worse. She prayed instead.

'Dear God, let him get over her. Dear God, let her not harm the baby. Dear God, let them believe me.'

But God seemed not to be listening. Luke went on loving Jenny, Jenny went on looking after Baby Emmy, and no one believed Christine when she said that Jenny was not to be trusted.

Christine had been married to Luke for nineteen years. She loved her husband with an energetic and consuming passion, well able to withstand his occasional adoration of passing girls. She would treat him, when he was thus enamoured, with a fond indulgence, saying, 'Well, men are like that, aren't they?' and waiting for common sense and reason to return, and uxorious content to shine once again from his gentle eyes. But Jenny was dangerous – Christine had suspected something unwholesome about her from the very first. In retrospect it was hard to tell, of course, quite when she had begun to think it – before Luke started mooning after Jenny, or after. But surely it was before – a sickly, chilly menace, a sudden shiver down the spine? Evil, the professor had written. Or perhaps he only wrote that, knowing what she wanted to hear? Americans were strange.

Even so, the damage was done. Now Christine feared for Luke, body and soul, and feared for Emmy, Lord Mader's baby daughter, even more. Jenny was Emmy's nanny. Little, pretty, safe words, adding up to something monstrous.

And of course if Christine murmured against Jenny, the other members of the staff assumed that Christine was jealous, and discredited what she said. Christine's husband, everyone knew, was in love with Jenny, trailing after her, gazing after her.

'But look,' Christine felt like saying, 'he's been in love a dozen times in as many years. It's just the way he is. I don't mind. He's a genius, you see. A mathematical genius, not one of your artistic geniuses, but a genius all the same. My feeling about Jenny is nothing to do with Luke's feeling for her.'

But the rest of the staff were dull, if good-hearted, and had their preconceptions about the world, which nothing now would shake: it was almost as if the chilly presence of Jenny had cemented in these preconceptions. Their vision narrowed to what they already knew. Christine concluded that Jenny had a strange deadening power over everyone, excepting only, for some reason, herself.

Jenny had a white, dead face and large, pale eyes she magnified with round owl spectacles, and short plain hair and a child's body. The face was thirty, the body was thirteen. Perhaps that was her power – the desire of the grown man for the pre-pubertal girl? A sickly and insidious love! And did the women perhaps remember themselves at thirteen and set Jenny free now, to do what they would have liked then?

Christine herself, at forty, was plump and maternal and pretty and busy. There could be nothing unhealthy in anyone's desire for her, and many did desire her, but she seldom noticed. She loved Luke.

Christine, the Doris Day of Mader House! Wonderful Mader House, Stately Home, giving the lucky villagers of Maderley full employment! With its Elizabethan chimneys, and Jacobean mullions, Georgian casements and Victorian tiles, it still remained imposing, if hardly gracious. Its lands and gardens, its ancient oaks, its Disneyland and zoo, its Sunday lunches with Lord and Lady Mader (fifty pounds a place-setting), made it popular with the millions. Lord Mader was often indisposed at these luncheons and his young brother Martin sent in his place, but the third Lady Mader, Mara, was always there. She was young and did as she was told, as did the villagers.

The Maders, their disparagers murmured, once a powerful and wealthy family, were now a handful of publicity-seeking degenerates. Even Christine, who loved to be loyal, increasingly saw truth in this observation. Yves, the present Lord, was thrice married. His first wife had been barren, and for that reason divorced. Lucien, son by his second wife, was a junkie, and Lucien's little sister Deborah now played the lead in skin-flicks. Yet these seemed matters of mirth rather than shame to Yves. A further son, Piers, was in real estate, and considered too boring for discussion. Left a widower by his second wife's suicide, Yves had promptly married Mara, a twenty-year-old Greek heiress, and sired little Emmy.

Yves had selected Jenny from over two hundred applicants

for the post of Nanny. He prided himself on being a good judge of character.

'Does he love the baby?' people would ask Christine. 'Oh yes,' she'd reply, adding in her heart, 'as much as he loves anything, which isn't very much.' The pressure of the words grew and grew and she was frightened that one day she would say them aloud.

'And the mother?'

'She's not very much at home, but I'm sure she does.' Christine was nice. She wanted to think well of everyone.

Mara loved treats and outings and hunting, and occasions on which she could wear a tiara, and the Mader family jewels – or, rather, their replicas. The originals had been sold in the thirties; and Maderley House itself would have followed in the fifties, had not Yves discovered that the people's fascination with their aristocracy could be turned to excellent financial account; whereupon he flung open the gates, and filled up the moat, and turned the stables into restaurants, and himself into a public show.

The show business side of Maderley was in Christine's charge – it was she who organised the guides, the cleaners, the caterers, even the vets for sick animals. She saw to brochures, catalogues and souvenirs. She took the takings to the bank. She had the status in the household of someone dedicated, who is despised for their dedication. She was underpaid, and mocked for being so by those who underpaid her, and did not notice.

Christine's husband Luke sat in the Great Library and worked out efficient mathematical formulae for the winning of the pools. Yves had once met, over dinner, a Nobel Prize winner, a mathematician, who had convinced him of the practicality of working out such formulae, computer-aided. Yves promptly had a computer-terminal installed in the Great Library, and Luke installed likewise. Visitors gawped at both between two and three on Wednesdays. Luke had a first-class honours degree in mathematics from Oxford. He had been a Maderley child with a peculiar gift for numbers and few social skills. He had returned to the village, married to Christine, a girl from far away, to write textbooks for graduates, which he did slowly, with difficulty, and for very little money.

The Great Library! There Christine fed the computer with data about visitors, gate takings, capital costs and so forth. And here Luke puzzled over his formulae, and here Jenny liked to sit in the winter sun beneath the mullioned windows, and rock the baby's pram, and watch Luke at work. The baby never cried. Sometimes it whimpered. The cover was pulled up well over its face.

Christine had tried to say something to Yves about Jenny and the baby.

'Yves' – his employees were instructed to call him by his Christian name – 'can I talk to you about Jenny?'

'What do you want to say?' He was unfriendly. She knew he did not like trouble. It was her function, after all, to keep it away from him. She had once asked for a rise in her wages, and the same shuttered, cold look had fallen across his face, as it now did, when she wanted to talk about Jenny.

'I don't think she's very good with the baby,' said Christine, tentatively, and wanted to go on and say, 'My Lord, I have seen bruises on the baby's arm. I don't like the way the baby whimpers instead of crying. I don't like the thinness of the baby's wrists. A baby's wrists should be chubby and creased, not bony.' But she didn't speak. She hesitated, looking at his cold face, and was lost.

'You mean she's too good with your husband, Christine,' was all Yves said. 'You sort out your own problems, don't come running to me.'

Christine, later that day, came across Yves with Jenny. They were together in the library. He had his hands on her thin shoulders: he, who seldom touched anyone. What were they saying?

Christine heard the baby make its little mewling cry, but Yves did not even glance into the pram.

Christine said to Mrs Scott the housekeeper. 'I'm worried about that baby. I don't think she gets enough to eat.'

Mrs Scott said, 'You don't know anything about babies. You've never had one. Jenny's a trained Norland nanny. She knows what she's doing.'

Jenny sat next to Mrs Scott at the staff lunch that day. They seemed very companionable.

Christine watched Luke watching Jenny being companionable with Mrs Scott, and the staff watched Christine watching Luke watching Jenny, and sniggered.

Christine telephoned the Norland nanny organisation, and they had no record of a Jenny Whitestone on their books.

Christine watched Jenny hold the baby's bottle an inch or so from the baby's mouth, so that the baby stopped whimpering and rooted with its mouth towards the warm, sweet smell and found it, and Christine watched Jenny tug out the bottle after the first few mouthfuls and put it back on the shelf. The baby moaned.

'What did you do that for?' asked Christine.

'I don't want the baby getting too fat,' said Jenny. 'It's a terrible thing to be fat.'

And Jenny eyed Christine's plump form with cold distaste.

Luke stopped making love to Christine altogether.

'It wouldn't be fair to you,' said Luke. 'How can I make love to you when I'm thinking of her? I wish I could, but I can't.'

'Why, why do you love her?' begged Christine.

But he didn't know, couldn't say.

It seemed to Christine that Luke felt cold in bed, as if his flesh was dying.

She spoke to the guides about Jenny, at their Monday morning meeting, where such things were discussed as meal breaks and the positioning of the silken ropes which guarded certain rooms and passages from the touch and view of ordinary people. 'Where did she come from?' Christine asked. 'Does anyone know?'

No one seemed to. It was as if she had always been there, along with the house itself, along with the family: the worm, or whatever it was, that nibbled away at the souls of the rich, so that born angels, they grew up devils.

For what could become of them but this? Generation succeeding generation: heartless mothers, distant fathers, and the distress of this made light of, by a surfeit of manners and money?

'The scale's all wrong,' Christine said in her heart. 'The house is just too big for people.'

Life's battles, life's events, triumphs and disasters – all were rendered puny by the lofty ceilings. Words of love and grief alike, hate and joy, all were muted beneath the arching vaults of the great hall, were sopped up and made one by ancient panelling. The stair was too high for the child to climb, or the old woman to descend. Marriages were lost in a bed so big it made passion trivial: the sexual act ridiculous under the cold eyes of ceiling cherubs. And animals! The love of dumb beasts put before the love of people; the death of a horse marking the year more than the death of a child; kennels always warmer than the nurseries. Manners replacing morals.

'They're born like anyone else,' Christine said in her heart, never aloud. 'And then I don't know what happens, but they end up monsters.'

So, now, it seemed to Christine, the damage which little Emmy could expect in the course of the next twenty years was being, at the hands of Jenny, inflicted upon her in as many months.

'I know why you love her,' she said presently to Luke, 'it's because she's the spirit of the House. And it's sickening and disgusting, and everyone loves it. Except me.'

'That isn't why I love her,' said Luke. 'And if you feel like that about the House, why go on working here?'

'What else could I do round here? There's no employment except at Maderley.'

But in spite of what she said, she stayed and she knew she stayed because she too, like Luke, was still under the spell of the Big House, and felt honoured by the company of Yves, whom she was privileged to call by his Christian name, and because she did not want to leave Emmy and Luke to the mercies of Jenny.

Lady Mara was due back from the Bahamas. The whole

house gleamed with polish and glowed with flowers.

But Emmy was listless, and blinked a good deal, and flinched and grizzled the day Lady Mara came back.

'She isn't very pretty,' said Mara, disappointed, peering into the pram, and after that seldom asked to see the child at all. She rode to hounds a good deal, along with farmers and carpet manufacturers.

'I wish you wouldn't,' complained Yves. 'Only the bourgeoisie go hunting these days.' But Mara was regaining her spirit, and learning how to do not what she was told, and she persisted, slashing at grasses with her riding crop, as if she'd like to slash at life itself.

Presently, Christine came across Jenny in the Great Library. Jenny had taken Emmy, for once, out of her pram. Jenny stood there, among ten thousand books, which were beautifully bound but never read, turning her owl eyes up to where the sunlight glanced through the windows, so that her spectacles dazzled, and seemed to retain the blinding shine even when she turned her head out of the sunlight to face Christine. Jenny, with her child's thighs in their tight, faded jeans, and budding breasts beneath a white T-shirt, and a dazzle where her face should be.

Jenny, with her soft, flat, slightly nasal voice, which could turn sharp and cruel and hard. Christine had often heard it. 'Christ, you little monster!' And slap, slap, thump, and then the weary grizzle again from Emmy.

Christine had never managed to get pregnant.

'Well,' the doctor had said, 'I dare say you have a child already, in your husband.'

Christine, cooking, nurturing, caring, worrying, had agreed with the doctor and not minded too much about their lack of children. Christine, after all, was the breadwinner. Perhaps what Luke saw in Jenny, suggested Christine, trying again, was his own unborn daughter? An incestuous love, given permission to live and thrive.

It was Yves who had given permission. Yes, he had.

'We all love Jenny,' Yves had said. 'Jenny saves us from our children.' Everyone except Christine, everyone's look said, watching Christine watching Luke watching Jenny, everyone loves Jenny.

Christine tried Yves' younger brother Martin, born by Caesarean while his mother lay dying from an overdose of sleeping pills and whisky, self-inflicted. Martin was the estate manager at Maderley. When Yves spoke to Martin it was in the same way he spoke to the upper servants – with a derisive politeness. Martin stuttered, so that Christine's conversation with him took a long time, and she was busy, needed at the toll-gate with new parking tickets.

'Sir, I don't think Jenny is what she says. She isn't a Norland nurse at all. I checked up.'

'No one round here is what they claim to be,' said Martin, sadly. 'And the baby is Lady Mara's business, not ours.'

'Couldn't you say something to Yves?'

'Not really,' said Martin. 'If you feel strongly about it, say something yourself.'

'I have, but he just got angry and wouldn't listen.'

'The baby looks like any other baby to me,' said Martin. 'Not that I know much about them, of course.' One of Martin's eyes turned inwards – a squint which had been left untreated in infancy, and so remained.

'Yves is a very good judge of character,' said Martin. 'If he employed Jenny she must be all right.'

The next day Christine saw Jenny wheeling the baby in the grounds, and Martin was with her. Even Martin! Martin, saying goodbye to Jenny, pecked her on the cheek, and she turned her face so that once again her glasses glinted and dazzled and the space beneath the pram hood seemed black, like the mouth of hell.

When Jenny wheeled the baby into the kitchen that day Christine bent to pick the baby up.

'Don't pick up the baby,' said Jenny sharply. 'She's sleeping quietly.' But to Christine the baby looked not so much asleep, as dead. And then an eyelash fluttered against the white cheek and Christine knew she was wrong. She went on counting sandwiches – two hundred ham, one hundred cheese – for the special Maderley tea, four pounds a head, served in the converted stable block.

'But *how* do you love her, *why* do you love her?'

She knew that she was nagging: she couldn't help it. She kept Luke awake at night now, working away at the truth. It was only while he slept that his body grew cold, and the pain of his answers was preferable to the chilly numbness of his sleep; she knew that, sleeping, he drifted off somewhere away from her, over the safe, surrounding walls of her love and, moth-like, floated towards the chilly, blinding light which used Jenny as its beacon.

It was at that time that she wrote to the professor of psychical research, and had confirmation of her fears. Jenny was evil.

'Lady Mara?'

'What is it, Christine?'

Lady Mara, broken arm in a sling – her horse had lurched and reared at nothing in particular, a sudden bright light in the grounds was all she could think of – was lately very much the grande dame. She would have bathed in asses' milk if she could.

'Lady Mara, I'm worried about the baby.'

'The baby is nothing to do with you. You look after the visitors and let Jenny look after the baby.'

Lady Mara was only twenty-one. The same age as Yves' daughter, the one who presented her body at rude, amazing angles for the benefit of the camera, a publisher and a million wistful men. But a title and wealth, and the assumption of power, of the right to tell other people what to do and what to say, add up to more than years. Mara stared coldly. Christine fumbled. Christine was impertinent. If she didn't stop meddling she might have to go. There were more than enough only too ready to take her place. Mara said nothing. There was no need to. Christine fell silent.

Yves and Mara went away to attend a wedding. Five thousand pounds, they had heard, were to be spent on flowers for the marquees alone. Who would miss a wedding like that?

Christine found her husband Luke weeping in the conservatory. 'What's the matter, Luke?'

But he was frozen into silence. Presently, he thawed, as if warmed by Christine's presence, her arm round his shaking shoulders, and spoke.

'I asked her. I plucked up courage and asked her. I said I wanted to sleep with her more than anything in the world.'

'And?' How cold the pit of the stomach, where words strike their message home.

'She laughed at me. She told me I was old and flabby. She said I was weak. She said I was a failure. Am I these things, Christine?'

'Of course not.'

'I love her more than ever.'

Christine went to see Jenny in her bedroom. 'You leave my husband alone,' said Christine, 'or I'll kill you.'

'Get him to leave me alone,' said Jenny, laughing, a cold, dead laugh. How could you kill what was already dead?

The baby murmured in its cot. Christine looked at little Emmy. Her eyes were black, and swollen. Christine lifted the baby out of its cot.

'You leave that baby alone,' snapped Jenny. 'You poor jealous, frustrated, barren, old bitch.'

It was the cry of the world, but it was not true. Christine's spirit was warm, loving and fecund.

Christine unwrapped little Emmy from her soft blankets and found that her back was bruised and her right leg hung oddly. Christine cradled the baby carefully in her arms and ran down long, long corridors, hung with family portraits, and down the great staircase, and into the reception area, where the tickets were taken, and rang all the bells she could, and Martin came, and Luke and three of the guides and Mrs Scott the housekeeper, and a cleaner; and Jenny followed after but stopped halfway down the stairs, in a little patch where the sun shone in, so she glowed all over, the source and not the reflection of light.

'Look,' said Christine, showing what was in her arms. Look! See what's she's done to the baby?'

'It was an accident,' called Jenny, in her soft, nasal voice. 'You're all my friends. You know I wouldn't do it on purpose.'

But the sun had shone in upon the wrong stair. She was just too far away, her voice just a little too faint. Jenny's words meant nothing to the cluster of people gazing at the baby, Lord Mader's baby, with its swollen eyes and its blue-black back.

'I'll get an ambulance,' said Christine.

'Think of the publicity,' said Martin, but he spoke without much conviction. 'Yves won't like it.'

'Perhaps we'd better telephone him and get permission,' said Mrs Scott.

'Let me take the baby,' called Jenny. 'It's me Emmy loves. You're all strangers to her. She'll get better if I hold her.'

And what Jenny said was true, but she couldn't make up her mind to lose the sun and step another stair down into the hall, and she faltered and was lost.

Martin rang Yves. Christine had his number: flicked through her efficient files and found it at once.

'Yves,' said Martin, stuttering his message out. 'You'd better come back here. The baby's got a bruise on its back. Christine thinks we should call an ambulance.'

'Christine would,' said Yves, sourly. 'Well, stop her. We'll be right back.'

But Christine called the ambulance all the same. They took the baby away and just as well, because Yves and Mara didn't return for three days.

Emmy had a fractured skull, two broken ribs, a broken thigh and a damaged kidney, but they patched her up quite well, and returned her after eight weeks looking quite pretty, so that her mother picked her up and murmured endearments and nuzzled into her baby neck, and fortunately Emmy smiled at that moment and didn't cry, which would have spoiled everything.

Christine lost her job, and Yves abandoned his hopes of breaking the Great Proletariat Pools Swindle and fired Luke too.

'You'd think they'd be grateful for my saving their baby,'

said Christine. 'But the upper classes are just plain twisted.'

'The Greeks used to kill the bearer of bad news,' said Luke, 'so think yourself lucky.'

The sight of the damaged baby had made him fall out of love with Jenny, and now he slept warm at night, and Christine beside him. Jenny did not lose her job, but at least she was no longer allowed to look after the baby. Instead, she did what Christine had been doing, for twice the money and with the help of an assistant.

'What a great judge of character Yves is!' said Christine sourly. Everyone she asked, and ask she did, everyone agreed with her. The Maders were degenerate and decadent. She could say the words aloud now, not just in her heart.

Later she heard that Jenny had taken another post as nanny to two little girls whose mother had died, and that Yves had written her an excellent reference.

'Your employees reflect back on you,' said Luke. 'That's what it is.'

Christine wondered whether to telephone the father of the two little girls and warn him, but knew she would never be believed. And perhaps, who was to say, there was someone like her in every little pocket of the world? Someone to save while others destroyed, or looked away. Wherever Jenny went, there would be someone like Christine.

'I loved her because she was evil,' said Luke, at last, explaining. 'She anaesthetised my moral nerve endings and that at the time was wonderful. And you were right, she was the spirit of the house.'

III

When We Dead Awaken

Ronald Duncan

I do not think I am more avaricious than most men; but the chance of obtaining something for nothing has always appealed to me. Especially when I could pick it with my own hands; blackberries, for these I will tear my clothes to pieces, nettle my face and hands, all for the pleasure of reaching the inaccessible something for nothing, and the pleasure of holding the plump fruit in my fingers. So, too, with mushrooms; as a child I began the search; and as a man, with less energy but the same incentive, I continue it. I will walk my friends' feet off to find a few more of those will-o'-the-wisp delicacies; and always there is a hope at the back of my mind that I will again find a complete mushroom ring, enough for a feast and to sell the rest as sheer profit. Such frail chances are strong ropes tethering many of us to pursuits and hobbies which, were we to consider the time we devote to them, would prove to us that it is impossible to obtain anything for nothing. And, as my wife has often reminded me, there is little profit in obtaining three pounds of wild fruit at the cost of a torn shirt and a large cleaning bill.

As the spring came round, I looked greedily across the beach to the great gaunt Cornish rocks where I knew the gulls would soon nest and lay their clutches of mottled blue and black eggs; to my taste a gull's egg is a delicacy, whereas a fowl's egg is just an egg.

And so, with my wife's blessing and a pair of old rubber shoes on, I set off with the privileged loan of her precious basket to the rock.

I knew every inch of the way and was soon scaling the precipitous surface which, being dry, seemed safe even to my nervous eye. Gulls scissored the air and sliced the sky and then would stay poised, and then fall and then rise. I kept my eyes to the rock and felt like a wood louse invading their pinnacle of a home. The top of the rock was relatively flat. I climbed on to my feet and eyed the ground for the precious eggs. To my disappointment I found only three where I had expected at least three dozen, though I saw scores of clumsily built, empty nests littered with the husks of my own seed corn. I could not allow myself to return with only three eggs; for there would be six of us to luncheon and I promised my wife that I could provide the *pièce de résistance* for that meal. On descending the rock I noticed that a great number of gulls circled a ledge of the main cliff some hundred feet above me. It was there, I supposed, that a friend of mine went for his eggs; for he always returned with a full basket and sold them for sixty pence a dozen, something for nothing. The cliff looked easy, that is, as easy as the rock I had already climbed. So, with my basket in my teeth, I began the ascent. Within ten minutes I was at the top, my basket full, it had been easy. I smoked a cigarette and admired the view, meditating on the pleasure the eggs would give my wife and wondering whether she would be able to preserve some for the winter. I had two pounds' worth of eggs; something for nothing, I was happy. I picked up my basket and then looked for my way down. But I could not see how I had managed to climb to where I now stood. I stood on a ledge of cliff four feet wide; at the back of me was an overhanging precipitous cliff which I knew it was impossible to scale. And each side of me a sheer drop of one hundred feet with the rocks and the sea's snarl at the bottom. In front, the ledge narrowed till it was a foot wide – no more than a plank – and on each side a sheer drop with nothing to hold on to.

Instantly, as though pricked by a hypodermic syringe, sharp panic spread over me and the sick fear of what lay before me settled in my throat as I realized what I had done. I had walked this narrow ledge, this one-foot plank, without noticing it, with my eyes searching for something for nothing;

I had managed to keep my balance over nothing. But now it was a different matter. My nerve had gone. I could not even stand where the ledge was comparatively wide. So I crawled inch by inch to where it narrowed and peered over. Each side was a sheer descent of slate-smooth rock. The ledge was less than a foot wide and more than five yards long. I must have crossed this without noticing it.

I knew I could not do it again.

I knew that I must do it again.

There was no other way, no other alternative. If only I could regain my nerve. I lit another cigarette and lay flat out, my hand holding a crack in the rock. My only chance was to make a run for it, with my eyes on some distant point, some imagined gull's nest. It could soon be over and, when it was, I swore in my panic to keep so many resolutions. I thought of my wife waiting for the eggs, and our laughing over my present predicament. Standing up, I threw my cigarette away and, with my eyes on a fixed point the other side, began to run towards the ledge, the sea almost meeting underneath it, the gulls swooping over it. I was on the ledge, my eyes still fixed on the point beyond it. In two seconds I would be across. A gull swooped towards me, my eyes lost their fixed objective, I hesitated ...

Then later I found myself sitting on the beach; I do not know how long I had sat there. I cannot tell; I may have dozed, I may have slept. The tide may have turned or the year turned. I do not know. I picked up my basket and walked up the path from the beach to the cottage. I thought of my wife waiting, the table laid, the guests' inconsequential chatter.

I put my basket behind my back and opened the door. The room was empty, there was no table laid. I went upstairs still carrying the basket of eggs. My wife lay on the bed. She was sobbing. I asked her what was wrong, she made no reply. Sobbing, she looked away from me. I begged her to tell me why she was crying. She made no answer. I put out my hand and touched her smooth, hot forehead. Instantly she screamed, rose from the bed and ran down the stairs out into the night. I followed, but could not find her. I returned to the empty house and went to my study and lay there, miserable and bewildered.

How long I slept there I do not know. The day may have drunk the night a dozen times for all I know; but when I awoke the stream still ran by the cottage. And I listened. My study is next to the sitting-room. Through the door I could hear voices and a fire crackling. It could not be the luncheon party, for we seldom light fires during May. I listened. My sister was there, she was serving coffee. My wife was there and there were two men with them; one was my neighbour, the other a friend of the family. Both people who would often drop in for an evening. I listened; my wife was no longer crying, the wireless was on. I opened the door slowly and went in; my neighbour sat in my chair, so I went over to the divan.

Nobody looked at me, nobody spoke to me and nobody passed me any coffee. They went on talking with the music playing.

My wife looked pretty; she went on knitting. What had I done to be left unnoticed?

I stood up and went to my wife's chair and on her lap placed the basket of gull's eggs. Her eyes rose slowly from her knitting and she screamed. 'Take them away, take them away!' she screamed, and ran from the room crying. My sister followed her. Then my friend said to my neighbour: 'Poor woman, she's still unnerved. That's the second time she's thought she's seen her husband carrying gulls' eggs ... She must go away.'

I went into the study. So I was dead, was I? When will we dead awaken?

IV

Escort

Daphne du Maurier

There is nothing remarkable about the *Ravenswing*, I can promise you that. She is between six and seven thousand tons, was built in 1926, and belongs to the Condor Line, port of register Hull. You can look her up in Lloyd's, if you have a mind. There is little to distinguish her from hundreds of other tramp steamers of her particular tonnage. She had sailed that same route and travelled those same waters for the three years I had served in her, and she was on the job some time before that. No doubt she will continue to do so for many years more, and will eventually end her days peacefully on the mud as her predecessor, the old *Gullswing*, did before her; unless the U-boats get her first.

She has escaped them once, but next time we may not have our escort. Perhaps I had better make it clear, too, that I myself am not a fanciful man. My name is William Blunt, and I have the reputation of living up to it. I never have stood for nonsense of any sort, and have no time for superstition. My father was a Nonconformist minister, and maybe that had something to do with it. I tell you this to prove my reliability, but, for that matter, you can ask anyone in Hull. And now, having introduced myself and the ship, I can get on with my story.

We were homeward bound from a Scandinavian port in the early part of the autumn. I won't give you the name of the port – the censor might stop me – but we had already made the trip there and back three times since the outbreak of war. The convoy system had not started in those first days, and the strain on the captain and myself was severe. I don't want you to infer that we were windy, or the crew either, but the North Sea in wartime is not a bed of roses, and I'll leave it at that.

When we left port, that October afternoon, I couldn't help thinking that it seemed a hell of a long way home, and it didn't put me in what you would call a rollicking humour when our little Scandinavian pilot told us with a grin that a Grimsby ship, six hours ahead of us, had been sunk without warning. The Nazi government had been giving out on the wireless, he said, that the North Sea could be called the German Ocean, and the British Fleet couldn't do anything about it. It was all right for the pilot: he wasn't coming with us. He waved a cheerful farewell as he climbed over the side, and soon his boat was a black speck bobbing astern of us at the harbour entrance, and we were heading for the open sea, our course laid for home.

It was about three o'clock in the afternoon, the sea was very still and grey, and I remember thinking to myself that a periscope wouldn't be easy to miss; at least we would have fair warning, unless the glass fell and it began to blow. However, it did the nerves no good to envisage something that was not going to happen, and I was pretty short with the first engineer when he started talking about the submarine danger, and why the hell didn't the Admiralty do something about it?

'Your job is to keep the old *Ravenswing* full steam ahead for home and beauty, isn't it?' I said. 'If Winston Churchill wants your advice, no doubt he'll send for you.' He had no answer to that, and I lit my pipe and went on to the bridge to take over from the captain.

I suppose I'm not out-of-the-way observant about my fellow-men, and I certainly didn't notice then that there was anything wrong with the captain. He was never much of a talker at any time. The fact that he went to his cabin at once meant little or nothing. I knew he was close at hand, if anything unusual should happen.

It turned very cold after nightfall, and later a thin rain began to fall. The ship rolled slightly as she met the longer seas. The sky was overcast with the rain, and there were no stars. The autumn nights were always black, of course, in northern waters, but this night the darkness seemed intensified. There would be small chance of sighting a periscope, I thought, under these conditions, and it might well be that we should receive no other intimation than the shock of the explosion. Someone said the other day that the U-boats carried a new type of torpedo, super-charged, and that explained why the ships attacked sank so swiftly.

The *Ravenswing* would founder in three or four minutes, if she was hit right amidships, and it might be that we should never even sight the craft that sank us. The submarine would vanish in the darkness; they would not bother to pick up survivors. They couldn't see them if they wanted to, not in the darkness. I glanced at the chap at the wheel; he was a little Welshman from Cardiff, and he had a trick of sucking his false teeth and clicking them back again every few minutes. We stood a pretty equal chance, he and I, standing side by side together on the bridge. It was then I turned suddenly and saw the captain standing in the entrance to his cabin. He was holding on for support, his face was very flushed, and he was breathing heavily.

'Is anything wrong, sir?' I said.

'This damn pain in my side,' he gasped. 'Started it yesterday, and thought I'd strained myself. Now I'm doubled up with the bloody thing. Got any aspirin?' Aspirin my foot, I thought. If he hasn't got acute appendicitis, I'll eat my hat. I'd seen a man attacked like that before; he'd been rushed to hospital and operated on in less than two hours. They'd taken an appendix out of him swollen as big as a fist.

'Have you a thermometer there?' I asked the captain.

'Yes,' he said. 'What the hell's the use of that? I haven't got a temperature. I've strained myself, I tell you. I want some aspirin.'

I took his temperature. It was a hundred and four. The sweat was pouring down his forehead. I put my hand on his stomach and it was rigid, like a brick wall. I helped him to his berth and covered him up with blankets. Then I made him drink half a glass of brandy neat. It may be the worst thing you can do for appendicitis, but when you're hundreds of miles from a surgeon and in the middle of the North Sea in wartime you're apt to take chances.

The brandy helped to dull the pain a little, and that was the only thing that mattered. Whatever the result to the captain, it had but one result for me. I was in command of the *Ravenswing* from now on, and mine was the responsibility of bringing her home through those submarine-infested waters. I, William Blunt, had got to see this through.

It was bitter cold. All feeling had long since left my hands and feet. I was conscious of a dull pain in those parts of my body where my hands and feet should have been. But the effect was curiously impersonal. The pain might have belonged to someone else, the sick captain himself even, back there in his cabin, lying moaning and helpless as I had left him last, some forty-eight hours before. He was not my charge; I could do nothing for him. The steward nursed him with brandy and aspirin, and I remember feeling surprised, in a detached sort of way, that he didn't die.

'You ought to get some sleep. You can't carry on like this. Why don't you get some sleep?'

Sleep. That was the trouble. What was I doing at that moment but rocking on my two feet on the borderline of oblivion, with the ship in my charge, and this voice in my left ear the sound that brought me to my senses? It was Carter, the second mate. His face looked pinched and anxious.

'Supposing you get knocked up?' he was saying. 'What am I going to do? Why don't you think of me?'

I told him to go to hell, and stamped down the bridge to bring the life back to my numbed feet, and to disguise the fact from Carter that sleep had nearly been victorious.

'What else do you think has kept me on the bridge for forty-eight hours but the thought of you,' I said, 'and the neat way you let the stern hawser drop adrift, with the second tug alongside, last time we were in Hull? Get me a cup of tea and a sandwich, and shut your bloody mouth.'

My words must have relieved him, for he grinned back at me and shot down the ladder like a Jack-in-the-Box. I held on to the bridge and stared ahead, sweeping the horizon for what seemed like the hundred thousandth time, and seeing always the same blank face of the sea, slate grey and still. There were low-banked clouds to the westward, whether mist or rain I could not tell, but they gathered slowly without wind and the glass held steady, while there was a certain smell about the air, warning of fog. I swallowed my cup of tea and made short work of a sandwich, and I was feeling in my pocket for my pipe and a box of matches when the thing happened for which, I suppose, I had consciously been training myself since the captain went sick some forty-eight hours before.

'Object to the port. Three-quarters of a mile to a mile distant. Looks like a periscope.'

The words came from the lookout on the fo'c'sle head, and so flashed back to the watch on deck. As I snatched my glasses I caught a glimpse of the faces of the men lining the ship's side, curiously uniform they were, half-eager, half-defiant.

Yes. There she was. No doubt now. A thin grey line, like a needle, away there on our port bow, leaving a narrow wake behind her like a jagged ripple. Once again I was aware of Carter beside me, tense, expectant, and I noticed that his hands trembled slightly as he lifted the glasses in his turn. I gave the necessary alteration in our course and took up my glasses once more. Now the periscope was right ahead, and for a few minutes or so the thin line continued on its way as though indifferent to our manoeuvre: then, as I had feared, the submarine altered course, even as we had done, and the periscope bore down upon us, this time to starboard.

'She's seen us,' said Carter.

'Yes,' I said. He looked up at me, his brown eyes troubled like a spaniel puppy's. We altered course again and increased our speed, this time bringing our stern to the thin grey needle, so that for a moment it seemed as though the gap between us would be widened and she would pass away behind us, but, swift and relentless, she bore up again on our quarter, and little Carter began to swear, fluently and passionately, the futility of words a sop to his fear. I sympathised, seeing in a flash, as the proverbial drowning man is said to do, an episode in my own childhood when my father lectured me for lying;

and even as I remembered this picture of a long-forgotten past I spoke down the mouth-tube to the engine room once more and ordered yet another alteration in our speed.

The watch below had now all hurriedly joined those on deck. They lined the side of the ship, as though hypnotised by the unwavering grey line that crept closer, ever closer.

'She's breaking surface,' said Carter. 'Watch that line of foam.'

The periscope had come abeam of us and drawn ahead. It was now a little over a mile distant, on our port bow. Carter was right. She was breaking surface, even as he said. We could see the still water become troubled, and then slowly, inevitably, the squat conning tower appeared and the long lean form rose from the depths like a black slug, the water streaming from its decks.

'The bastards,' whispered Carter to himself, 'the filthy, stinking bastards.'

The men clustered together below me on the deck watched the submarine with a strange indifference, like spectators at some show with which they had no concern. I saw one fellow point out some technical detail of the submarine to the man by his side, and then light a cigarette. His companion laughed and spat over the side of the ship into the water. I wondered how many of them could swim.

I gave the final order to the engine-room, then ordered all hands on deck to boat stations. My next order would depend on the commander of the submarine.

'They'll shell the boats,' said Carter. 'They won't let us get away, they'll shell the boats.'

'Oh, for God's sake,' I began, the pallor of his face begetting in me a furious senseless anger, when suddenly I caught sight of the wall of fog that was rolling down upon us from astern. I swung Carter round by the shoulders to meet it. 'Look there,' I said, 'look there,' and his jaw dropped and he grinned stupidly. Already the visibility around us was no more than a cable's length on either side, and the first drifting vapour stung us with its cold, sour smell. Above us the air was thick and clammy. In a moment our after-shrouds were lost to sight.

I heard one fellow strike up the opening chorus of a comic song in a high falsetto voice, and he was immediately cursed to silence by his companions. Ahead of us lay the submarine, dark and immobile, the decks as yet unmanned and her long snout caught unexpectedly in a sudden shaft of light. Then the white fog that enveloped us crept forward and beyond, the sky descended, and our world was blotted out.

It wanted two minutes to midnight. I crouched low under cover of the bridge and flashed a torch on to my watch. No bell had been sounded since the submarine had first been sighted, some eight hours earlier. We waited. Darkness had travelled with the fog, and night had fallen early. There was silence everywhere, but for the creaking of the ship as she rolled in the swell and the thud of water slapping her sides as she lay over, first on one side, then the other. Still we waited. The cold was no longer so intense as it had been. There was a moist, clammy feeling in the air. The men talked in hushed whispers beneath the bridge. We went on waiting. Once I entered the cabin where the captain lay sick, and flashed my torch on to him. His face was flushed and puffy. His breathing was heavy and slow. He was sleeping fitfully, moaning now and again, and once he opened his eyes, but he did not recognise me. I went back to the bridge. The fog had lifted slightly, and I could see our forward-shrouds and the fo'c'sle head. I went down on to the deck and leant over the ship's side. The tide was running strongly to the south. It had turned three hours before, and for the fourth time that evening I began to calculate our drift. I was turning to the ladder to climb to the bridge once more when I heard footsteps running along the deck, and a man cannoned into me.

'Fog's lifting astern,' he said breathlessly, 'and there's something coming up on our starboard quarter.'

I ran back along the deck with him. A group of men were clustered at the ship's side, talking eagerly. 'It's a ship all right, sir,' said one. 'Looks like a Finnish barque. I can see her canvas.'

I peered into the darkness with them. Yes, there she was, about a hundred yards distant, and bearing down upon us. A great three-masted vessel, with a cloud of canvas aloft. It was too late in the year for grain-ships. What the hell was she doing in these waters in wartime? Unless she was carrying timber. Had she seen us, though? That was the point. Here we were, without lights, skulking in the trough of the sea because of that damned submarine, and now risking almost certain collision with some old timber-ship.

If only I could be certain that the tide and the fog had put up a number of miles between us and the enemy. She was coming up fast, the old-timer, God knows where she found her wind – there was none on my left cheek that would blow out a candle. If she passed us at this rate there would be fifty yards to spare, no more, and with that hell-ship waiting yonder in the darkness somewhere the Finn would go straight to kingdom come.

'All right,' I said, 'she's seen us; she's bearing away.' I could only make out her outline in the darkness as she travelled past abeam. A great high-sided vessel she was, in ballast probably, or there would never have been so much of her out of the water. I'd forgotten they had such bulky afterdecks. Her spars were not the clean things I remembered either; these were a mass of rigging, and the yards an extraordinary length, necessary, no doubt, for all that bunch of canvas.

'She's not going to pass us,' said somebody, and I heard the blocks rattle and jump, and the rigging slat, as the great yards swung over. And was that faint high note, curious and immeasurably distant, the pipe of the boatswain's whistle? But the fog vapour was drifting down on us again, and the ship was hidden. We strained our eyes in the darkness, seeing nothing, and I was about to turn back to the bridge again when a thin call came to us across the water.

'Are you in distress?' came the hail. Whether her nationality was Finnish or not, at least her officer spoke good English, even if his phrasing was a little unusual. I was wary, though, and I did not answer. There was a pause, and then the voice travelled across to us once more. 'What ship are you, and where are you bound?'

And then, before I could stop him, one of our fellows bellowed out: 'There's an enemy submarine come to the surface about half-a-mile ahead of us.' Someone smothered the idiot a minute too late and, for better or worse, our flag had been admitted.

We waited. None of us moved a finger. All was silent. Presently we heard a splash of oars and the low murmur of voices. They were sending a boat across to us from the barque. There was something furtive and strange about the whole business. I was suspicious. I did not like it. I felt for the hard butt of my revolver, and was reassured. The sound of oars drew nearer. A long, low boat like a West Country gig drew out of the shadows, manned by half-a-dozen men. There was a fellow with a lantern in the bows. Someone, an officer I presumed, stood up in the stern. It was too dark to see his face. The boat pulled up beneath us and the men rested on their oars.

'Captain's compliments, gentlemen, and do you desire an escort?' inquired the officer.

'What the hell!' began one of our men, but I cursed him to quiet. I leaned over the side, shading my eyes from the light of the boat's lantern.

'Who are you?' I said.

'Lieutenant Arthur Mildmay, at your service, sir,' replied the voice.

There was nothing foreign in his intonation, I could swear to that, but again I was struck by his phraseology. No snottie in the Navy ever talked like this. The Admiralty might have bought up a Finnish barque, of course, and armed her, as Von Luckner did in the last war, but the idea seemed unlikely.

'Are you camouflaged?' I asked.

'I beg your pardon?' he replied in some surprise. Then his English was not so fluent as I thought. Once again I felt for my revolver. 'You're not trying to make a fool of me by any chance, are you?' I said sarcastically.

'Not in the least,' replied the voice. 'I repeat, the captain sends his compliments, and as you gave him to understand we are in the immediate vicinity of the enemy, he desires me to offer you his protection. Our orders are to escort any merchant ships we find to a port of safety.'

'And who issued those orders?' I said.

'His Majesty King George, of course,' replied the voice.

It was then, I think, that I felt for the first time a curious chill of fear. I remember swallowing hard. My throat felt dry, and I could not answer at once. I looked at the men around me, and they wore, one and all, a silly, dumb unbelieving expression.

'He says the King sent him,' said the fellow beside me, and then his voice trailed away uncertainly, and he fell silent.

I heard Carter tap me on the shoulder. 'Send them away,' he whispered. 'There's something wrong; it's a trap.'

The man kneeling in the bows of the gig flashed his lantern in my face, blinding me. The young lieutenant stepped across the thwarts and took the lantern from him. 'Why not come aboard and speak to the captain yourself, if you are in doubt?' he said.

Still I could not see his face, but he wore some sort of cloak round his shoulders, and the hand that held the lantern was long and slim. The light that dazzled me brought a pain across my eyes so severe that for a few moments I could neither speak nor think, and then, to my surprise, I heard myself answer: 'Very well, make room for me, then, in your boat.'

Carter laid his hand on my arm. 'You're crazy,' he said. 'You can't leave the ship.'

I shook him off, obstinate for no reason, determined on my venture. 'You're in charge, Carter,' I said. 'I shan't be long away. Let me go, you damn fool.'

I ordered the ladder over the side, and wondered, with a certain irritation, why the stupid fellows gaped at me as they obeyed. I had that funny reckless feeling which comes upon you when you're half-drunk, and I wondered if the reason for it was my lack of sleep for over forty-eight hours.

I landed with a thud in the gig and stumbled to the stern beside the officer. The men bent to their oars, and the boat began to creep across the water to the barque. It was bitter cold. The clammy mugginess was gone. I turned up the collar of my coat and tried to catch a closer glimpse of my companion, but it was black as pitch in the boat and his features were completely hidden from me.

I felt the seat under me with my hand. It was like ice, freezing to the touch, and I plunged my hands deep in my pockets. The cold seemed to penetrate my greatcoat and find my flesh. My teeth chattered and I could not stop them. The chap in front of me, bending to his oar, was a great burly brute, with shoulders like an ox. His sleeves were rolled up above his elbows, his arms were bare. He was whistling softly between his teeth.

'You don't feel the cold, then?' I asked.

He did not answer, and I leant forward and looked into his face. He stared at me as though I did not exist, and went on whistling between his teeth. His eyes were deep set, sunken in his head. His cheekbones were very prominent and high. He wore a queer stovepipe of a hat, shiny and black.

'Look here,' I said, tapping him on the knee, 'I'm not here to be fooled, I can tell you that.'

And then the lieutenant, as he styled himself, stood up beside me in the stern. 'Ship ahoy,' he called, his two hands to his mouth, and, looking up, I saw we were already beneath the barque, her great sides towering above us. A lantern appeared on the bulwark by the ladder, and again my eyes were dazzled by the sickly yellow light.

The lieutenant swung on to the ladder and I followed him, hand over fist, breathing hard, for the bitter cold caught at me and seemed to strike right down into my throat. I paused when I reached the deck, with a stitch in my side like a kicking horse, and in the queer half-light that came from the flickering lanterns I saw that this was no Finnish barque with a load of timber, no grain-ship in ballast, but a raider bristling with guns. Her decks were cleared for action, and the men were there ready at their stations. There was much activity and shouting, and a voice from for'ard calling orders in a thin, high voice. There seemed to be a haze of smoke thick in the air, and a heavy sour stench, and with it all the cold dank chill

I could not explain.

'What is it?' I called. 'What's the game?' No one answered. Figures brushed past me, shouting and laughing at one another. A lad of about thirteen ran by, with a short blue jacket and long white trousers, while close beside me, crouching by his gun, was a great bearded fellow like my oarsman of the gig, with a striped stocking cap upon his head. Once again, above the hum and confusion, I heard the thin, shrill piping of the boatswain's whistle and, turning, I saw a crowd of jostling men running barefooted to the afterdeck, and I caught the gleam of steel in their hands.

'The captain will see you, if you come aft,' said the lieutenant.

I followed him, angry and bewildered. Carter was right, I had been fooled; and yet, as I stumbled in the wake of the lieutenant, I heard English voices shouting on the deck, and funny unfamiliar English oaths.

We pushed through the door of the afterdeck, and the musty rank smell became sourer and more intense. It was darker still. Blinking, I found myself at the entrance of a large cabin, lit only by flickering lantern light, and in the centre of the cabin was a long table, and a man was sitting there in a funny high-backed chair. Three or four other men stood behind him, but the lantern light shone on his face alone. He was very thin, very pale, and his hair was ashen grey. I saw by the patch he wore that he had lost the sight of one eye, but the other eye looked through me in the cold abstracted way of someone who would get his business done and has little time to spare.

'Your name, my man?' he said, tapping with his hand upon the table before him.

'William Blunt, sir,' I said, and I found myself standing to attention with my cap in my hands, my throat as dry as a bone, and that same funny chill of fear in my heart.

'You report there is an enemy vessel close at hand, I understand?'

'Yes, sir,' I said. 'A submarine came to the surface about a mile distant from us, some hours ago. She had been following us for half-an-hour before she broke surface. Luckily the fog came down and hid us. That was at about half-past four in the afternoon. Since then we have not attempted to steam, but have drifted without lights.'

He listened to me in silence. The figures behind him did not move. There was something sinister in their immobility and his, as though my words meant nothing to them, as though they did not believe me or did not understand.

'I shall be glad to offer you my assistance, Mr Blunt,' he said at last. I stood awkwardly, still turning my cap in my hands. He did not mean to make game of me, I realized that, but what use was his ship to me?

'I don't quite see,' I began, but he held up his hand. 'The enemy will not attack you while you are under my protection,' he said. 'If you care to accept my escort, I shall be very pleased to give you safe conduct to England. The fog has lifted, and luckily the wind is with us.'

I swallowed hard. I did not know what to say.

'We steam at eleven knots,' I said awkwardly, and when he did not reply I stepped forward to his table, thinking he had not heard. 'Supposing the blighter is still there?' I said. 'He'll get the pair of us. She'll blow up like matchwood, this ship of yours. You stand even less chance than us.'

The man seated by the table leant back in his chair. I saw him smile. 'I've never run from a Frenchman yet,' he said.

Once again I heard the boatswain's whistle, and the patter of bare feet overhead upon the deck. The lanterns swayed in a current of air from the swinging door. The cabin seemed very musty, very dark. I felt faint and queer, and something like a sob rose in my throat which I could not control.

'I'd like your escort,' I stammered, and even as I spoke he rose in his chair and leant towards me. I saw the faded blue of his coat, and the ribbon across it. I saw his pale face very close, and the one blue eye. I saw him smile, and I felt the strength of the hand that held mine and saved me from falling.

They must have carried me to the boat and down the ladder, for when I opened my eyes again, with a queer dull ache at the back of my head, I was at the foot of my own gangway, and my own chaps were hauling me aboard. I could just hear the splash of oars as the gig pulled away back to the barque.

'Thank God you're back!' said Carter. 'What the devil did they do to you? You're as white as chalk. Were they Finns or Boche?'

'Neither,' I said curtly. 'They're English, like ourselves. I saw the captain. I've accepted his escort home.'

'Have you gone raving mad?' said Carter.

I did not answer, I went up to the bridge and gave orders for steaming. Yes, the fog was lifting, and above my head I could see the first pale glimmer of a star. I listened, well content, to the familiar noises of the ship as we got under way again. The throb of the screw, the thrash of the propeller. The relief was tremendous. No more silence, no more inactivity. The strain was broken and the men were themselves again, cheerful, cracking jokes at one another. The cold had vanished, and the curious dead fatigue that had been part of my mind and body for so long. The warmth was coming back to my hands and feet.

Slowly we began to draw ahead once more, ploughing our way in the swell, while to starboard of us, some hundred yards distant, came our escort, the white foam hissing from her bows, her cloud of canvas billowing to a wind that none of us could feel. I saw the helmsman beside me glance at her out of the tail of his eye, and when he thought I was not looking he wet his finger and held it in the air. Then his eye met mine, and fell again, and he whistled a song to show he did not care. I wondered if he thought me as mad as Carter did. Once I went in to see the captain. The steward was with him, and when I entered he switched on the lamp above the captain's berth.

'His fever's down,' he said. 'He's sleeping naturally at last. I don't think we're going to lose him, after all.'

'No, I guess he'll be all right,' I said.

I went back to the bridge, whistling the song I had heard from the sailor in the gig. It was a jaunty, lilting tune, familiar in a rum sort of way, but I could not put a name to it. The fog had cleared entirely, and the sky was ablaze with stars. We were steaming now at our full rate of knots, but still our escort kept abeam, and sometimes, if anything, she drew just a fraction ahead.

Whether the submarine was on the surface still, or whether she had dived, I neither knew nor cared, for I was full of the confidence which I had lacked before and which, after a while, seemed to possess the helmsman in his turn, so that he grinned at me, jerking his head at our escort, and said, 'There don't seem to be no flies on Nancy, do there?' and fell, as I did, to whistling that nameless jaunty tune. Only Carter remained aloof. His fear had given way to sulky silence, and at last, sick of the sight of his moody face staring through the chartroom window, I ordered him below, and was aware of a new sense of freedom and relief when he had gone.

So the night wore on, and we, plunging and rolling in the wake of our escort, saw never a sight of periscope or lean grey hull again. At last the sky lightened to the eastward, and low down on the horizon appeared the streaky pallid dawn. Five bells struck, and away ahead of us, faint as a whisper, came the answering pipe of a boatswain's whistle. I think I was the only one that heard it. Then I heard the weak, tired voice of the captain calling me from his cabin. I went to him at once. He was propped up against his pillows, and I could tell from his face he was as weak as a rat, but his temperature was normal, even as the steward had said.

'Where are we, Blunt?' he said. 'What's happened?'

'We'll be safely berthed before the people ashore have rung for breakfast,' I said. 'The coast's ahead of us now.'

'What's the date, man?' he asked. I told him.

'We've made good time,' he said. I agreed.

'I shan't forget what you've done, Blunt,' he said. 'I'll speak to the owners about you. You'll be getting promotion for this.'

'Promotion my backside,' I said. 'It's not me that needs thanking, but our escort away on the starboard bow.'

'Escort?' he said, staring at me. 'What escort? Are we travelling with a bloody convoy?'

Then I told him the story, starting with the submarine, and

the fog, and so on to the coming of the barque herself, and my own visit aboard her, not missing out an account of my own nerves and jumpiness, either. He listened to me, dazed and bewildered on his pillow.

'What's the name of your barque?' he said slowly, when I had finished.

I smote my hand on my knee. 'It may be Old Harry for all I know; I never asked them,' I said, and I began whistling the tune that the fellow had sung as he bent to his oars in the gig.

'I can't make it out,' said the captain. 'You know as well as I do there aren't any sailing ships left on the British register.'

I shrugged my shoulders. Why the hell couldn't he accept the escort as naturally as the men and I had done?

'Get me a drink and stop whistling that confounded jig,' said the captain. I laughed, and gave him his glass.

'What's wrong with it?' I said.

'It's *Lilliburlero*, centuries old. What makes you whistle that?'

I stared back at him, and I was not laughing any longer. 'I don't know,' I said, 'I don't know.'

He drank thirstily, watching me over the rim of his glass. 'Where's your precious escort now?' he said.

'On the starboard bow,' I repeated, and I went forward to the bridge again and gazed seaward, where I knew her to be.

The sun, like a great red globe, was topping the horizon, and the night clouds were scudding to the west. Far ahead lay the coast of England. But our escort had gone.

I turned to the fellow steering. 'When did she go?' I asked.

'Beg pardon, sir?' he said.

'The sailing ship. What's happened to her?' I repeated.

The man looked puzzled, and cocked his eye at me curiously. 'I've seen no sailing ship,' he said. 'There's a destroyer been abeam of us some time. She must have come up with us under cover of darkness. I've only noticed her since the sun rose.'

I snatched up my glasses and looked to the west. The fellow was not dreaming. There was a destroyer with us, as he said. She plunged into the long seas, churning up the water and chucking it from her like a great white wall of foam. I watched her for a few minutes in silence, and then I lowered my glasses. The fellow steering gazed straight in front of him. Now daylight had come he seemed changed in a queer indefinable way. He no longer whistled jauntily. He was his usual stolid seaman self.

'We shall be docked by nine-thirty. We've made good time,' I said.

'Yes, sir,' he said.

Already I could see a black dot far ahead, and a wisp of smoke. The tugs were lying off for us. Carter was in my old place on the fo'c'sle head. The men were at their stations. I, on the captain's bridge, would bring his ship to port. He called me to him, five minutes before the tugs took us in tow, when the first gulls were wheeling overhead.

'Blunt,' he said, 'I've been thinking. That captain fellow you spoke to in the night, on board that sailing craft. You say he wore a black patch over one eye. Did he by any chance have an empty sleeve pinned to his breast as well?'

I did not answer. We looked at one another in silence. Then a shrill whistle warned me that the pilot's boat was alongside. Somewhere, faint and far, the echo sounded like a boatswain's pipe.

V

Seven Ghosts In Search

Fred Urquhart

Which ghostly part will I play today? Will I be Cordelia or Beatrice? Or will I be a Merry Wife being a bawd to some of our primmer visitors who remember that Ellen was a Dame Grand Cross of the British Empire?

It is the hottest afternoon of the hottest summer, and I am tired. Even though the heat cannot affect me physically any more – if someone like me can be called physical – I have not the heart to do much. I am getting so old. I was born in 1847, so what does that make me? My memory has got so bad, I need Marguerite Steen here to help me out, as she helped me that awful week in Manchester in – was it 1921? I know it was the steamiest week of a very steamy July, several years before I became a ghost altogether. I was engaged to give Shakespeare readings between films at the Gaiety Theatre that had been turned into a cinema. Such a vulgar programme, but perhaps they hoped to make it less vulgar by having poor old Ellen Terry in it.

I would never have contemplated it, but Edy said we needed the money. After all, it was a hundred and fifty pounds for the week, and that seemed a great deal. Edy was to have come with me, but she was ill, and Marguerite took her place. Dear Marguerite, she was a godsend. She nursed me through the whole long wretched week, prompting me when I forgot my lines – which was oftener than I care to think. The manager was so pleased with her for propping old Ellen up that he gave her a cigarette case. Silver was it? Expensive I know. Where is that cigarette case now? Marguerite herself is haunting somewhere in Spain looking for the shades of her matador and Sir William Nicholson.

In Manchester, between the Pathe Gazette and a dreadful comedy film – Chester Conklin or somebody – I did the 'mercy' speech. Shall I do it now for these two American tourists gazing at my stage costumes through the glass wall? What are the opening lines? Maybe if I step into Portia's scarlet robes it will help me remember ... Something about mercy ... Ah! The quality of mercy is not strained.

'God have mercy on us! Hank! The dummy's moving! It has a woman's face, and she's smiling at me. Do you see her, Hank? It's a spook!'

Silly creature. What does she expect? If she visits Ellen Terry's house, even if it has been turned into a museum, does she not expect to see some ghosts?

Look at these people hurrying to find why that fool is making all the fuss. A pity they would not slip and fall on that uneven polished passageway, as I so often slipped until I got too old to hurry and crawled along holding onto the wall. But I am being uncharitable. They have paid their money and must be entertained. They are the audience and as long as they applaud, or seem to applaud, by appreciating my former possessions, I must appreciate them.

Will I give them another ghostly showing now I have stepped out of Portia's legal robe? I wander among my other costumes displayed on the dummies. Will I be Ophelia? But no, let us leave that until I go outside, then I shall float on top of the scummy canal-like stream that runs beside the garden. Edy always called it 'the river' but it is not broad enough, not wild enough, not abandoned enough to be a real river.

Will I be Ellen playing Juliet? While the visitors look through the glass wall, and her husband tries to pacify that screaming woman – poor man, I feel so sorry for him – shall I step into Juliet's shoes and show them the magic of old Verona?

Or is it Lady Macbeth, the dark one, the forlorn one, the mad one, the visitors would like to see? Oh, my loves, which one of you shall I be? Where are all of you now, the parts I used to play? Not in these gossamer-thin stage costumes that would crumble at a touch stronger than that of ghostly old Nell.

I shall go downstairs and stroll in the garden.

There is a coachload of blue-rinsed ladies outside the gate. Are they coming in? Is entrance to the Museum part of their conducted tour? They are gawking at the house and giggling to each other. Shall I show myself? Shall I play the part of Dame Ellen Terry receiving guests at her farmhouse at Smallhythe in Kent? Shall I make this the most memorable day of their limited suburban lives? What would they do if they saw old Ellen in her regency-striped pink and mauve dress rising from the sunny haze of the garden?

That was what I was wearing one day when a coach like this – only much smaller, what used to be called a charabanc – with a similar contingent of gossip-hungry women stopped at the gate. Even in those days this was a common enough occurrence. I always went inside and hid whenever a charabanc appeared. But that day I couldn't hide. Already I was sitting in the pony-trap with Edy beside me holding the reins. 'Bow to them, Mother,' she said. 'Bow!' And so I did what I was told, and Edy whipped up the pony and away we high-stepped to Tenterden to do the weekly shopping. I sat beside Edy on the green leather cushion with one hand clutching my large pink straw hat, the one with violets sewn all over the brim, though there was really no need to hold, for a mauve tulle motoring veil was keeping it firmly in place.

In Tenterden Edy drew up the pony with a flourish in the middle of the street, opposite the grocer's. You could do that in those days, there was so very little traffic. And she shouted: 'Ahoy there, Mr Sidebotham! Mr Sidebotham!' And she cracked the whip several times and little Mr Sidebotham came running. He had strands of dyed black hair glued across his brown bald skull, and he smoothed them down even more as he stood beside the trap, bowing and saying: 'Good afternoon Miss Craig. Good afternoon, Miss Terry madam. And what can I do for you this fine afternoon, Miss Craig?'

After Edy had given him the order she shouted for the butcher. He was waiting; he catapulted out as soon as she shouted: 'Ahoy there, butcher!' And once again we heard the chorus: 'Good afternoon, Miss Craig. Good afternoon, Miss Terry madam.' They always called me 'Miss Terry madam.' I found this rather irritating.

That was a few years before I was made a Dame. I wasn't made one until 1925 and so, seeing I died in 1928, I hadn't long to enjoy being called 'Dame Ellen'. I should have been made a Dame much earlier. I would have been if my friend Queen Alexandra had had anything to do with it. She was a nice woman and a real friend. But it wasn't politic in those days to make actresses Dames of the British Empire. Genevieve Ward was the first. In 1921. Who remembers Genevieve Ward now? I should have been made a Dame at the same time, but I was passed by although my name was a household word.

It grieved Edy much more than it grieved me. She was a curious girl, Edy. Always a strange one. The servants were more in awe of her than they ever were of me. Or of my dearest Ted, even though he must have appeared strange enough, for I once heard one of them say: 'Mr Gordon Craig's a proper coughdrop with 'is sombrero and 'is long black cloak.' But Edy – they never called her 'Miss Edy'. She was always given the benefit of the full 'Miss Edith'. I did not know she was a lesbian until after I was dead. How could I? People did not talk then about lesbianism, even the ones who knew about it. I knew Edy was odd, of course; I knew there was something fishy about the great friendship between her and that girl who called herself Christopher St John, the one who helped Edy to write *Ellen Terry's Memoirs*. I never really liked that girl St John. I didn't like the book either. She wasn't the girl I would have chosen to be my ghost. I preferred Marguerite Steen, and I told her: 'You must write all this after I'm dead. You must make a picture of all of us.' And that is what she did. She wrote a very good book about the whole family, *A Pride of Terrys*. Old Ben would have been very proud of it and the raggle-taggle race he spawned.

Bugger it, I manifested too late! The blue-rinsed gapers have gone.

I learned that word from Ben, who had quite a flow of picturesque expressions. He used them along with his slipper when we were children and did not learn our lines or enunciate words properly. Ben disapproved of anything slipshod. He would have considered this manifesting too late to be bad stage-management.

A pity I was not on cue. There is nobody here now to see old Nell in her regency-stripe. So many motors are parked along our road that the coach has had to go as far as the bridge to find a place. I shall go there and be Ophelia madly dying. That will give the blue-rinsed ladies a treat. I say ladies rather than women, for they give such genteel, comic ladylike squeaks when they look over the bridge and see me floating on the scummy green stream.

I wave up to them and cry: 'There's fennel for you, and columbines; there's rue for you; and here's some for me; we may call it herb of grace o' Sundays. O! you may wear your rue with a difference. Sweet ladies.'

Perhaps they already rue the cost of their coach tour? So that will make up for it. That will make them remember their visit to Ellen Terry's house. I wish Henry had been here to give them his gloomy Hamlet glower and declaim, while he held my head: 'That skull had a tongue in it, and could sing once.' The gapers would then have had their money's worth. Two stars for the price of one. Even though I was sometimes overshadowed by Henry at the Lyceum – only because his parts were longer and his lines more abundant – we were good partners. Dear Henry, I miss him.

In the dining room there are only a few visitors. The one who attracts me most is a tall young man with shoulder-length golden hair, perfectly straight and shed in the middle, giving him an almost prissy look. He wears a very dark business suit, and his hands are clasped behind his back as he marches – there is no other word for his brisk military movements – from one exhibit to the next. He looks at them with an impassive face. He is looking now at the portrait of Sarah Bernhardt. I wonder who he is and what has brought him here. Is he an actor? Is he a BBC producer? I wish he had someone with him so that I might hear his voice. Voices mean so much to me. Has he come here as a Terry admirer? Or was he just passing and come in to spend an idle hour? Or is he hoping to pick up a girl? He looks lonely. I shall show myself to him.

As I was when I was sixteen. The tomboy Nelly with what Charles Reade used to say was my 'harvest-coloured hair', my big hands and my big feet, and wearing the brown silk dress I wore when I married old George Frederick Watts. I still wonder what made me marry 'The Signor', as that malevolent woman Prinsep always called him. He thought about nothing but his painting, and Mrs Prinsep encouraged him. That nasty woman who was responsible for separating us. But I forgot Mrs Prinsep long ago – if I still don't forgive her. And I forgot Watts too. Let him stick to his old canvases and the drip at the end of his nose. All I want to remember is that everybody said then that Nelly Terry was a romp.

'Excuse me, sir, can I help you? You look lost. Perhaps I could guide you round the exhibition? I am very familiar with the place. I am Mrs G.F. Watts. I was billed as that before I was divorced from Watts – you may perhaps have seen the famous portrait he painted of me? I was furious because I meant no name to be as famous as that of Ellen Terry, but the management insisted.'

Whatever is the man saying? Gabble, gabble, gabble. Sounds like German or Russian. Double Dutch to me, anyway! He gives me a jerky bow, unclaps his hands and marches out of the door. Oh dear, you backed a loser that time, Nelly. Obviously the one man who does not think Nelly is great fun.

I shall go upstairs and see what response I get there. It is my duty to appear to my public. Somebody said once – was it Bernard Shaw? – that I was an actress who needed to be seen as well as heard. I am beginning to feel like one of Pirandello's six characters in search – of what? Satisfaction? Perfection? Or the real Nelly Terry?

A family is crowded against the glass wall of the costume room. The father is a big man, very broad, wearing a white shirt and tight fawn trousers. Rather a handsome man, distinguished-looking. The mother is a little wax doll nonentity, and her arm is clamped firmly into the man's while she gazes up at him. My costumes mean nothing to her. They have two daughters, big and fair and cowlike, aged maybe twelve and thirteen, wearing bathing costumes that hardly cover them decently. Also a boy of nine or ten, very slim and dark, quite unlike his sisters. He is good-looking and wears nothing but a pair of briefs. For a moment I think I have strayed onto Brighton beach. I can almost hear the cries of the hokey-pokey man and the deck-chair attendant. The girls are pressing so tightly against the glass that their noses are squashed, making them more pudding-faced than ever. They will grow up to be like their mother. The boy stands back, aloof and silent, but he is taking in everything.

One girl says: 'Dad, what're we lookin' at all them old dresses for? Dad, why did we come into this creepy old place? When're we gunner Camber Sands?'

'Yes, Dad, when're we gunner 'ave chips?'

The boy says nothing. He eases his briefs and lets them slap back against his moist brown skin.

Old Ben Terry, that purist of language, would have slippered these girls. I think of manifesting as Lady Macbeth sleep-walking to give them a fright. But they are not worth it. I content myself by slapping each girl on her bottom. They do not even move. As I pass him I caress the boy's back. He looks over his shoulder, but his aloofness does not waver.

There are only two people in the Library. Two middle-aged men who are not together and obviously don't want to know each other. It is extraordinary that the Library should be the least visited room in the house. Of course, few people read nowadays; they are too busy watching television. That would never have done for me. I loved to have books on the shelves, taking them out and looking at them. Not that anybody can do that here. The National Trust has fenced my books in behind immovable glass. A reasonable precaution, of course. Otherwise they would become tattered by mishandling and also perhaps get stolen.

I stand beside the man looking at the telegrams and letters in the glass case in the middle of the room. He is reading a letter inviting me to visit her little mountain home and ending 'Best love and bless you, Nellie Melba.'

I materialise beside him wearing the lavender muslin dress I wore at Melba's home that time I was on a lecture tour in Australia. Dear Melba, she was a marvellous woman, but a bit of a trial sometimes. I always appreciated her most when she was singing.

'Good afternoon,' I say.

He looks at me over his half-moon glasses and says: 'Didn't notice you coming in. Come by helicopter, ha? Might have. One minute nobody, the next you're here. Do I know you? Seems to me I've seen you before. Face is very familiar.'

'My face is all over this house, sir,' I say and vanish.

I hover in the Lyceum Room watching the ebb and flow of visitors. Some examine everything closely, standing long before each exhibit. Some hurry through, glancing only briefly while talking all the time to their companions. I would like to sit down, but two old women are sitting on my day-bed, although a notice says it is not to be touched. Will I frighten them off? No. I will be charitable; they are dazed like myself by the heat.

My attention is diverted by a handsome young man looking at the bill advertising my 50th anniversary on the stage in 1906 in *Captain Brassbound's Conversion*. With James Carew as my leading man. Bold brash James with his face like a Red Indian's. Not indeed unlike this young man.

'Tell me, sir, are you interested in the work of Mr Shaw? Or are you interested in Ellen Terry? Have you seen any recent production of *Brassbound*? If so, I should be interested to hear who played my part?'

The young man – he is much bigger than James Carew but as magnetic – backs away a step at the sight of Ellen, nearly sixty years old, in Lady Cicely Waynflete's black velvet gown. 'Ellen Terry,' he whispers. 'I never expected to meet your ghost.'

'And why not, sir? If you come to my house, you must expect to find me – in spirit, anyhow.'

'I am honoured, Dame Ellen. I'm so honoured that I can't believe it's true. I must be dreaming ... but oh, what a magnificent dream!'

'You're a sweet young man,' I say, and I touch his cheek with my lips before I drift through the wall into my bedroom.

Certainly a much sweeter young man than my third husband, James Carew, the Red Indian from Indiana. James and I didn't last long. When he kicked my dog it was a good excuse to get rid of him.

The afternoon is almost over. The visitors are thinning out. Yet there are more in my bedroom than I care for at nearly five o'clock. Here are big fair Dad and his wife and family. I thought they had gone long ago to Camber in search of chips. Little wifie and those two blonde hockey-players don't have as big a grip on Dad as they think. The dark good-looking boy moves silently behind them. Like Dad, he looks closely at the large paintings of my mother, Sarah, and Edy and Ted as children. He reads the telegrams from Queen Alexandra and George V. Then he moves to the schooldesk where my children were taught their lessons. And he sits down.

What is he thinking of, this aloof boy with the brooding eyes? Is he thinking that he too will go on the boards? Does he see himself as a Laurence Olivier or a John Gielgud of the future? Who knows what is going on inside that dark head? I sit beside him and say: 'I was about your age – I was nine – when I made my debut as Mamillius in *The Winter's Tale* on the 28th April 1856. It was a fine occasion, not only for me but for the whole company, for we acted in the presence of Queen Victoria and Prince Albert. I should have been nervous but I wasn't. I wasn't at all nervous of the Queen, who smiled and waved at me from her box when I made my bow. I was much more nervous of Charles Kean and his wife Ellen Tree. Even though she was my namesake I was terrified of Mrs Kean. I was with the Kean Company for three years – years that were too often punctuated by Mr Kean ringing a handbell every time one of the actors did something that displeased him.'

'Where did that little gal come from, Hank? Oh my God! Don't tell me it's another spook!'

That stupid American woman again. I thought she had gone long ago. She is spoiling what is perhaps my most rewarding encounter of the day. This boy has imagination and will never forget our meeting. A pox on that woman! I stick out my tongue at her before I vanish, giving the dark boy a reassuring pat on the head. I know that he knows I have planted a seed that will flower.

I am tired; I have manifested seven times, and that is enough for one day. The audience is going. As the curator ushers out Dad and his family and Hank and his wife, the dark boy looks towards the corner where I am standing, unseen to all the rest, and he smiles.

I smile back to him and bow. 'Farewell, boy, may the gods be kind and let you do what you wish.' Then I look at the photograph of the young man on the wall beside me, the photograph inscribed 'To Ellen Terry with love from Siegfried Sassoon.'

And so I settle on my bed to while away another night in the realm of the dead, and I will recite Siegfried's poem *Grandeur of Ghosts* if I can remember the lines:

When I have heard small talk about great men
I climb to bed; light my two candles; then
Consider what was said ...
How can they use such names and be not humble?
The dead bequeathed them life; the dead have said
What these can only memorize and mumble.

VI

Act of Contrition

James Turner

'I could never have cut the tree for the Cross,' Peter said whenever anyone questioned him about his love of wood.

'But you're not a Christian! What's the Cross to you?'

'You miss the point,' Peter would push his hand through his red hair, a worried look on his face and in his blue eyes. He always had difficulty in explaining the simplest things. 'It's not the Cross itself, though that's ghastly enough. It's the actual wood to make it. I couldn't have hurt it.'

'Rubbish!' his friends exclaimed. He infuriated them by being so ridiculous and passionate about the beauty of oak and ash, of walnut and mahogany, that he refused even the simple chore of cutting logs. 'Where would we be if everyone felt like you do? Hurting wood! Never heard of anything so absurd. And, after all, your father was a superb craftsman, a real genius of a wood carver. He was famous. I mean, his things fetch the earth today. So why be so utterly silly?'

'You don't understand,' Peter replied, knowing it was useless trying to get through to them. 'I'm not like him at all. For one thing I'm too big, I'm clumsy. I would only hurt the wood, I know it. My father, since you've brought him up, thought me a fool or even worse.'

He thought of his father who had frequently thrashed him for his stupidity. Peter bore the punishments with fortitude, but they did not make him like his father. In the end, what he hated most of all about him, was his sarcasm. The odd thing was that if he got hold of a chunk of wood, some piece which someone else had cut, say a chog discarded by his father, he would polish it to perfection. Nox and apple he worked on till the grain shone, and merely for the pleasure of handling; teak sent him into raptures.

At such times he seemed to be in touch with something he could not describe, something beyond him, coming to him from the wood, brought out in him by the polishing. If he had been put to it – and he would never have thought of mentioning it to anyone, least of all his father – he would have said that the polished wood was reality, that something beyond the ordinary day-to-day events and thoughts which people take for reality.

'Oh, God,' he exclaimed, 'my friends will think I'm round the bend if I dare to tell them that on top of my feeling about hurting wood. Real crackers!' Yet he could not deny the thrill which ran up his spine. The live timber of trees gave him an almost sexual delight like certain lines of poetry which made his hair stand on end when he repeated them.

He first came to understand his love of wood when his father, determined to make a craftsman of him, insisted that he take carpentry, as an extra, at his preparatory school, in Sussex. Peter, too young to be able to realise what was being asked of him, attended the wood-working class. Because he was, at this age, a boy who did what he was told (things were much easier this way), he agreed to try to make a sewing box as a present for his mother, to be given to her on the first day of the holidays. It was a simple enough job. He botched it hopelessly. He could not understand why, as he worked, tears were constantly falling down his cheeks. He did his best to hide them from the other boys, who laughed at him.

Mr Thomas, the carpentry master, who came in to teach for two afternoons a week, was aware that something was wrong when the screwdriver with which Peter was trying to screw in the hinges of the lid, slipped and cut his left hand. He sent him to the Matron. When he returned he called him over to a corner of the carpentry shop and spoke to him.

'You'll never make a carpenter, you know, Peter, not as long as you live,' he said, brushing his large tobacco-stained moustache, pushing his steel-framed spectacles to the top of his head. 'It just doesn't seem to be in you. Look at this dovetailing.' He turned the sewing box in his rough hands. 'I've done my best but this box of yours is frightful. And these screws, they're not even in straight. I daresay,' he smiled down at Peter, 'I daresay you hate the work, don't you?'

'It's not that, sir. I'd like to be as good as my father, but I don't seem ...'

'Ah, him!' Mr Thomas cut Peter short, sighed and looked into the distance through the windows of the shop, out to the playing fields and the woods beyond. 'We'd all like to be as clever as your father. We all know how good he is, all of us in the trade, that is. He's a genius, I always say, a genius, born not made.'

'Yes, sir. But it's, it's ...'

'Well, my boy, what is it?' The old man put out his hands and touched Peter on his bare arm. The action gave the boy confidence. He felt that Mr Thomas would not scoff; he might even understand.

'It's just,' he said, almost in a whisper, 'it's just that I hate hurting wood. That's all I'm doing, sawing and planing and banging in nails. I know it's silly, sir, but, you see, when my father does it, it's as if the carving was already there and all he did is to make the wood happy by releasing it. Besides, he thinks such an idea as hurting wood is silly, the sort of idea that a woman would have.'

Mr Thomas did not jump down Peter's throat, he didn't even exclaim 'rubbish!' He smiled and took a pipe out of his green working apron. 'Oddly enough,' he said, looking earnestly at the boy. 'I do know how you feel. Wood's too precious to mismanage. It does have a life of its own, you can feel it. I'm with you there. But as to hurting it? Well, don't you think that would have occurred, if at all, when the tree was first cut down? That was the time for pain, not now, not here in the workshop.'

'Yes, sir, perhaps you're right. But I still think, I still feel, every time ...'

'The best thing for us to do, then, is to finish the box so as not to disappoint your mother.' Mr Thomas could see that the cut in Peter's hand was not as bad as he first thought and that the plaster was efficient. Neither did he, being paid so much per pupil, want to lose Peter till the end of term. 'And then we'll see. Perhaps when your father sees what you've made of it, he'll understand that you'll never be any good. Come along, I'll give you a hand.'

Peter returned to the hideous article he was making with loathing. It was, nevertheless, no small thing to him that Mr Thomas agreed with him. At least, partially. And, in some unexplained way, the fact that his blood was still on the wood comforted him. Now the wood and himself were one, suffering together.

So Peter completed the term because he trusted Mr Thomas and came to rely on him, more and more, at every lesson. Besides the sewing box Mr Thomas, trying to wean him from what he privately considered to be very odd ideas, persuaded him to construct a bookcase. Neither was even competently made, simple as they were. The hinges of the sewing box were screwed in all wrong and, to make the thing more farcical, it was made from too heavy deal to start with. It had all the appearance of a pregnant woman, too full in the middle. The bookcase had one shelf not straight; books put on it always slipped sideways.

When his father saw the monstrosities he flew into a rage, picked up the sewing box and hurled it against the wall. It was so strong that it did not break, leaving a hole in the wall paper. But his mother gathered it up again and, because she adored her son, praised the result of the extra lessons and, later, at spring-cleaning, hid the 'treasures' in the attic where they remained virginal and unlooked-at in their appalling coat of brown varnish.

Yet one night, during the first week of his holidays, his father, relenting perhaps of his anger, called Peter into his workshop where he was in the middle of carving an intricate set of candlesticks.

'I'd like to show you something,' he said, in a last effort to instruct his son. 'It's my earnest desire that you follow me and become a craftsman. If you pay attention to me you'll never make such rubbish as that sewing-box again. I'll teach you all

I know and, perhaps, you'll be famous one day, too.'

Peter, afraid of his father, and not liking to tell him that Mr Thomas had suggested that he give up carpentry altogether, did as he was bid. He went into the workshop innocent. When he left he was already a young man, aware of the possibilities of evil within him.

His father's chisels were lying bright and gleaming on their green baize cloth, at least thirty of them, of all sizes and curious shapes for gouging wood. They were immaculate, precise and sharpened to the last hair's breadth. His father, whose pride they were, reached for a narrow instrument, like a surgeon reaching for a scalpel. He pressed it hard into the grain of the oak and drew forth a thin squirl of wood. An intricate curve of the utmost delicacy and beauty was formed which instantly gave meaning and subtle light to the surface of the wood. The chisels were working as if by superhuman agency. The beauty of the gleaming edges held a fascination for Peter. He could not take his eyes from them. He was too young yet to realise the temptation they were offering him. But tense and alarmed at himself without knowing why, he screamed. As his father placed the chisel once more into the wood, he fled from the workshop, shouting, 'No, no, it's too cruel. I can't bear it. I won't bear it.'

That night he dreamed of wood squirming under his father's hands, pleading for mercy, but with no escape. He began to hate his father. What he did not realise was that his father began to hate him, a hate which would not die with his death.

It was inevitable that anyone so gentle as Peter should choose to live in the country. It was inevitable that he should fall in love with Chrissie, a country girl; it was inevitable that she should adore him.

Her love for Peter survived even the interview she had with his father, when he told her that Peter was a clumsy fool, had no training for anything, would never be able to support her, and that all he was good for was cleaning out public lavatories. Chrissie flew into a rage and defended Peter.

Act of Contrition 65

'He's, he's got something you'll never have,' she almost shouted at the old man, 'for all your carving and, and, your genius. He can love, not just me or the next person, but everything, even you, if you'd let him. Yes, even you, for all your cruelty,' and she fled from the room, her father-in-law's laughter echoing in her ears.

Now, ten years after that scene – both Peter's father and mother were dead – he and Chrissie were living in a large, many-roomed Georgian house in Kent. The place was much too big for them, but it was all Peter could afford these days, when people were going in for smaller houses and only large, awkward ones were available at all cheaply.

He called himself a naturalist and did occasionally have articles printed in London papers dealing with wild life, particularly butterflies. His chief pleasure was watching badgers in their hundred year's old set in the wood not far from the house. He did all he could, by writing and protesting, to defend them against the local farmers who, imagining the badgers to be pests, hunted and killed them most cruelly.

From being a large boy he was now a large man. His red hair was wiry and ungovernable; from this alone it might have been supposed that he had a fierce temper. The truth was the exact opposite. If anything he was too easily persuaded, and gave into Chrissie almost as soon as she opened her mouth. Nothing was too good for her. Had he been pressed he would have died for her.

It was his hair which appealed most to Chrissie, who was small and determined, efficient and very much aware of Peter's love for her. Indeed, had she not been efficient they would have found it very hard to exist on the little Peter made and his small legacy.

And it was when Chrissie, who knew of Peter's attitude to wood and rather made light of it, thinking like many women that she was divinely appointed to 'save' her husband from his eccentricities, and completely unaware of evil, began asking for extra bits of furniture to fill the empty house, that the trouble began.

'I need a little tea trolley,' she said sweetly, 'It really would be useful. You know, the kind of thing on light wheels which I could push about.' She was seeing herself, then, elegantly attired in an afternoon frock, crossing the hall of the large house, pushing the small trolley on which were her silver teapot, cream jug and cake stand, wedding presents which she had never used, since they mostly ate in the kitchen. She would even make Maids-of-Honour and delicate coconut pyramids ...

'Can't you buy one?' Peter brought her back to earth.

'But, darling,' she smiled wanly, 'we can't afford such luxury, you know that. It would be so easy for you to do it. Think how happy you'd make me.'

Only later he knew that he should have been firm from this moment. Hating to upset her, to disappoint her, to see her sad in any way, he allowed himself to give in to what he did not, then, recognise as temptation. 'I don't know, dear. It's a job for an expert cabinet-maker. My father, for example. He'd have made you a beauty.'

'But he's dead, Peter. Don't talk nonsense. I'm sure it's only because you're lazy. Something of your father's talent must have come down to you.'

'You know perfectly well what I feel about wood.'

'Nonsense!' she pretended to be annoyed. 'That was a lot of childish nonsense. I'm surprised to hear a grown man talk like that. Besides you make yourself absurd with your religious attitude, for that is all it is, where a bit of old wood is concerned. Besides,' she added winningly, 'I'll come into the loft over the stables, now and then, to see how you're getting on. Who knows, you might be so successful that we could set up a small country industry and undercut the big stores.' Wild dreams were, once again, flitting through Chrissie's head. She was determined to drive Peter to the idea.

'I'd botch the thing,' Peter said, hesitatingly, 'I don't suppose you ever saw the sewing box and bookcase I made when I was a boy, did you?'

'Actually, I did.' Chrissie smiled gently, already in her mind bossing it over a few workmen in Peter's workshop, having converted the entire range of stables and lofts into a 'factory'. 'Your mother and I were in the attic of your old home one day, just before the house was sold, and she showed me. I thought them rather sweet.' With such words she unwittingly drove another nail into Peter's coffin.

'They were horrible. The sort of thing which even now gives me nightmares. I wake up sweating with horror when I think of them.'

'I'm sure you'd do better today,' Chrissie persisted. Neither of them was aware of the influence beyond them both. They were too fixed in the material of their living to be conscious of any lingering influence from the dead, or for the chances they were giving to such influences. It was just possible that Peter might yet draw back, for in one of those flashes of intuition or whatever it is called, he thought he saw the face of his father looking in at the kitchen window. Of course such a 'vision' was absurd, but it so happened that Chrissie was talking about him, and this must have made the mental idea of his father take on some kind of shape.

'Especially as you inherited all those wicked chisels and other tools from your father. And it's not as if you'd have to buy any wood. There's a pile of it in the loft which we took over when we came, all ready for you. Why let it rot when you could make use of it, without any expense whatever?'

'Father was an expert wood-carver. He was and is famous.'

'Exactly!' Chrissie drove on, quite unaware of what she was doing. 'And, for all your silly ideas about the sacredness of wood, you never threw those chisels away, did you? Why not? Don't you think you're a bit of a hypocrite?'

Peter twisted and turned in his chair. He looked at the window again, but no one was there. And yet, when she mentioned the chisels his father's face *had* been extremely vivid to him. 'No, I don't,' he shouted. 'I won't have you call me that. Do you hear, I won't have it.'

'I'll call you what I like,' she got out, rapping the table with her fists in anger. 'You're nothing but a lazy great lout who could earn a decent living if he tried and give me a few nice things like other wives have.' Chrissie was aghast at what she was saying and quite unable to stop herself.

Peter had risen from his chair, his great hands held out before him. 'So that's what you think of me? A useless lout?'

'Yes, and like your father said, only capable of cleaning out public lavatories.'

'You little bitch! Trust you to side with him.'

The words brought Chrissie to her senses. How could she have been so cruel to him? But it was too late. Peter, in case he should be mastered by his anger, went out, crossed the stable yard, and up the wooden stairs to the loft. Chrissie, wise enough not to follow him, dissolved into tears, afraid of the anger she had seen in his eyes. Yet, for all their quarrel, she was convinced that those massive wrists and arms should be put to some better use than looking at birds and insects or holding her, so lovingly, in bed. She was, above all, a woman of principle, unable to conceive that a man like Peter could ever be afraid.

He had forgotten, if he had ever known, how delightful was the feel of the wooden handles of the chisels his father had left him in his will. It half soothed his inner anger. Wicked was, of course, the right word to describe their gleaming, razor-sharp blades.

He took them out of the green baize cloth in which they had reposed ever since his father last used them, all the time aware of his own excitement, of his anger with Chrissie, and of something else, an odd light in the corner of the loft over the stables. He thought it was a reflection of sunlight from the acacia tree outside, and thought no more about it. He was quite unconscious that his lips were drawn back from his mouth in a kind of snarl. He'd show her, that he would, he was damned if he'd have her call him names.

The chisels were, suddenly, like weapons in his hands, subtle extensions of his fingers, springing alive in the large space of the loft. It might now, then, have been too late if his father's face had not suddenly sprung up in his mind, due to Chrissie's words. She should not have brought him up. He had been a hatchet-faced man, silent, dark and big like his son. Peter had never thought of him as cruel, not even when he beat him. Yet it was with these brilliant, yes, cruel, tools that he worked in wood the most delicate shapes, flowers, birds, trees, in exquisite intaglio.

If it had not been for Chrissie saying that he was only fit to clean out lavatories, there might still have been time for him. If he could have flung the chisels across the loft into the centre of that odd light, and so swept away his anger with her, this might have been all right. But the feel of the handles was too great a temptation. He'd show her, by God he would. After all, he loved wood and those wooden handles were exquisitely moulded to fit the hand, his father's hand, and now his. They might have been made for him. What real harm could there be in placing the gleaming blade against wood, just to see if perhaps he had been wrong all the time and his father's skill had come down to him?

His rage died in him, as the chisel handles soothed him. So, in a second, he laid himself fully open to temptation as an alcoholic might say, 'there's no harm in just taking one.' The battle was lost.

But something else was urging him on. A feeling of power was coming from the chisels themselves. He did not realise, then, that their immaculate edges, like perfect lines of poetry, were doing something horrible to him. He was conscious, at the last moment, and before he gave way to seduction, of great fear and personal danger. Yet in the bright evening light he suddenly knelt beside the heap of timber, planks, two-by-twos which Chrissie had mentioned. His eyes filled with tears. A sob rose in his throat as his right hand, almost as if it were being directed, went out and grasped the naked wood.

The temptation was too great for him. His tears could not drive away the hideous feeling of pride in his heart, pride driving him on to be as great as his father; jealousy of his father's fame; admiration for the perfection of the chisels; visions of the mockery of his friends who regarded him as soft; his memory of Chrissie's scorn and his anger with her. On top of that, the subtle temptation of his old schoolmaster's words, 'the damage was done when the trees were cut down. Then was the time of pain.' The voice was coming to him from the light in the corner of the loft, burning with a steady brilliant flame, corrosive, dangerous. He waited, turned, and distinctly heard his father say, 'I'll teach you everything I know. You'll be famous, too.'

Anger still burned in him, though now it was anger not so much at Chrissie, but at his own weakness. He began to heave up the wood and mark it with the flat carpenter's soft lead pencil which had also been his father's. It seemed to be speaking to him in its smooth line across the wood as if it had been waiting all these years to draw such a line and was now released.

He shut his eyes at the first cut of the saw, at the wriggling wood under his left hand. He almost gave in then, not caring if Chrissie did think of him as a lout and useless. But the light in the corner of the loft moved. It not only bathed Peter's hand with the saw in it, it fell with extreme brightness on the thirty fine heads of the chisels. Now there was a glory about them which he could no longer resist. Some hand was already lifting one of them, holding it out to him. The evil power of the chisels was calling out to him to be used. He was lost, his anger and pride submerged him.

The beauty of his past love of wood went down, in a moment, in a fit of sadistic pleasure. It was almost as if the wood were feminine, were Chrissie in her scorn and anger, and resisting him. Determined to get every possible satisfaction from his shame at succumbing to temptation, he shouted out, as if it were at Chrissie, 'Stay still damn you, stay still,' and fixed the wood in a vice on the work-bench which was also part of his father's legacy. The wriggling wood lay inert. Peter was breathing deeply. He was trembling and, as he cut and shaped the wood as he had seen both his master and his father do it, he began to laugh. So deep was his concentration on his evil pleasure that he was unaware of the hand, issuing once more from the light in the corner, directing him.

That night, after had had made it up with Chrissie, he was almost brutal in his love-making. Chrissie struggling against him (as the wood had struggled) wondered what devil she had aroused.

He knew now – and did not care – that the spirit of his father was directing him. He knew the location of this spirit (Chrissie would have called it a ghost, but it was more than that) was the light in the loft which never left the tips of the chisels. It was into this light that he entered each time he went to the loft, into the power of his father now too great for him to resist. And once having given in to the temptation of the chisels there was no going back. He began to fall into self delusion. He could see no fault in the tea trolley he was making. To him it was a superb creation, the legs cut and incised with a design of flowers and leaves which was hopelessly amateur. If, as he now knew, his father was directing him, the thing must be good.

In fact it was a monstrosity which needed the help of a man from the village to get it down into the kitchen, where it stood in all its unpainted hideousness, rather like the funeral car of the Duke of Wellington which was so big and heavy that it got stuck in the mud going up Ludgate Hill to St Pauls. You could have carried a complete dinner for twelve on its three shelves.

Chrissie stood aghast at the monster. Expecting a delicate tea trolley, she did not know how to react to the arrival of a kind of railway buffet (admittedly without its urn) into her life. She turned away, uncertain whether to laugh or cry, and stammered out her disappointment, just as his mother had with the sewing box, 'Lovely, dear, exactly what I wanted. But isn't it just a little too ...'

Her words were drowned by Peter's excited remarks. It was enough that she was apparently pleased. 'Now for the bed. You did say you wanted me to make a double bed, didn't you? I agree, we've been in those single ones too long. Right, I'll be getting back to the loft, then. It will have the most beautifully carved legs and headpiece. Just you wait.'

Chrissie's eyes were staring out of her head when she turned from the stove on which she was cooking a ham. Not Peter, but his father was standing in the doorway. She choked back a scream and, without a word, the apparition had gone through the door into the yard. She moved, controlled herself into thinking that what she had seen was really Peter, who did resemble his father, she told herself. She crossed to the trolley which had already taken over the kitchen with its implacable presence. She got out, 'Oh, no, no, no.'

She held out a hand, gingerly touching the fearful trolley which was the result both of her enthusiasm and the genius and hate of her father-in-law. She began to laugh hysterically. What ghosts had she caused to rise, what ghosts were even now directing Peter's hands? And yet the trolley, in its hideousness, denied the fact of what she had seen. If what she had seen was Peter's father, there in the kitchen doorway, there in Peter's body, then he could not have made so hideous an object. Nor had she the least idea of Peter's sin, his giving in to pride and the longing for fame, of the grossness of his denial of what had been his truth, of which this trolley was the outward sign.

In the half light she thought the monstrosity took on a life of its own. It was about to attack her. She shoved it violently into a corner and broke into tears. The trolley banged the wall hard and brought down a plate from the beautiful Welsh dresser nearby, which smashed into pieces at her feet.

Nothing could now stop Peter. He was engrossed in his desire. A fever to build was on him and only in his mind, disguised the other desire – a lust really – to clamp wood into the vice, to have it, which he had so loved once, powerless for him to cut and hack at. With renewed vigour and, at times, with sweat pouring from him he attempted the refinement of carving the square old oak beams he had found lying in a barn on the property, into the shape of legs for the double bed.

The chisels encouraged him, leaping in his hands as if put there, living in the cuts in the wood, singing in the appallingly ugly gouges he was making. To him they were beautiful; his whole body responded to the inertness of the wood. At times he laid his bare chest and stomach on the wood itself to take its vibrations into his blood. All the time the light in the corner of the loft increased until it, at last, enfolded him whenever he was working.

With the deception of a perfection he was performing, his lovemaking demands on Chrissie became more overpowering. In other ways, too, he was changing from the gentle character she had married into a masterful, overbearing person so like the father she remembered. She shrank away from the sight of his red hair (now flaming) and his massive wrists when he came into meals. He took to tearing his food, swallowing it quickly and going off into the empty bedrooms, his eyes glowing, his red hair sizzling, it seemed, with a kind of static electricity, deciding what he would build when the bed was done. He was never really happy, now, unless his hands were on his father's chisels. From loving wood so much, he had turned to a lust for the chisels, saws, hammers and wrenches. It was not too much to say that all wood, even trees in the garden which he was cutting down for future use when they should mature, was now his victim.

Still he was no carpenter and certainly no wood carver. If, as Chrissie was convinced, his father was informing his hand, his mind, he was not having much luck. The gift was not being passed on. The bed finished, the problem was twofold. It was far too big to move in one piece, and far too wide for a spring mattress foundation. He solved the first problem by taking it, bit by bit, into the house. As he was erecting it in the room Chrissie wanted, she followed, fearfully. She was shrinking away from him.

'Peter,' she begged, almost in tears, 'it's going to be as big as the Great Bed of Ware.'

He grinned at her, his teeth showing. 'That's right,' he said. 'Just you wait till I've got it up. Just you wait till tonight.'

The second problem, the base on which to put the mattress, he solved by going into the attics and ripping up the old foot-wide oak floor boards. The pulling out of the century-old nails kept him happily engaged the whole morning, his strength mastering their stubborn rustiness. When, in the afternoon, Chrissie returned from her shopping (it was still steak, very rare, that Peter wanted) the bed was finished. It stood like an apron stage of a theatre flaring at her, wide and long with a head slightly higher than its foot, another masterpiece of inexactitude and futility. In fact, it was immoveable.

That night, on the three mattresses laid sideways and the six double sheets needed to cover them, Chrissie had the most horrible nightmares. She was convinced that it was not Peter making love to her, but his father. She woke shrieking, and knew that she would have to go away.

Her going made no difference to Peter. He was still engrossed in the dark delight of his lust. He merely ate at the village pub and went straight back to the loft over the attics.

The first sign of the end came one afternoon when he took the huge wardrobe he had been working on for some time, into the house and erected it. Anyone could have seen, by the tightness of his lips, the brilliance of his blue eyes and his unkempt red hair, that the strain was beginning to tell on him.

As he was driving in one of the screws to the wardrobe, the screwdriver slipped and gashed his left hand in the palm, almost in the exact spot where he had cut himself at school all those years ago. The odd thing was that the wound hardly bled at all. Swearing, Peter went to pick up the tool. It slipped away from him across the floor. He went after it. It snaked away again as if it were trying to escape his huge hands. Savagely Peter flung out a boot and caught the screwdriver against the wainscot. There was a squeaking noise which he put down to mice. Later he was not so sure.

He gripped the screwdriver hard and finished assembling the wardrobe. It took all his strength to master the reluctance of the tool to work properly. He had no idea that nature and all natural things and creatures had, at last, revolted against him and his pleasure in cruelty.

When Chrissie wrote to ask if he were all right and would he like her to come back to him, he replied in a letter of great, almost mad ecstasy.

'I've built it all. The bed, the wardrobe, a desk for my study, two chests for blankets and things and three tables. All are inside the house which is now no longer empty. I am making a set of dining room chairs. All are exquisitely carved. Father is proud of me. The chisels have triumphed.'

Chrissie, trembling, fully understood what he meant. She could not return to him. She knew that whatever he had made was hideous, and that he was still suffering under the delusion of thinking himself a master carver. She recognised, only too clearly, that it was not her, but his father's dead spirit (if it were dead?) which was driving him on. 'Dead, dead, dead,' she screamed. 'You can't hurt him.' But she knew that it could. She longed, at this distance, to save him. How was she to know that the saviour, who always comes, but is not always recognised, was to arrive from quite another quarter and would have nothing to do with her?

Summer was almost over when, in the dusklight of an early October evening, Peter was standing at the door of the loft. He wasn't doing anything, yet he was conscious of the bright chisels behind him, the stacks of newly delivered timber and the pile of leftovers from the wood he had already murdered. He was looking into the top branches (so high up was the loft) of the acacia tree which had, so far, escaped his frenzy of felling. A wood pigeon alighted at the moment the setting sun struck between the leaves of the tree, now beginning to turn colour.

As it settled and began to utter its soft plea, 'Don't cry so Susan, don't cry so, Susan,' Peter felt a sharp pain in his left hand where, a week before, he had gouged it with the screwdriver. The pain brought his head up and he looked directly into the tree, into the eye of the grey bird. It was bowing gracefully to him.

The pain was now unbearable. He began to run about the loft swearing and in agony. At the sharpest hurt, the whole palm of his hand seemed to burst open and pour out dark blood. It was spurting over everything, across the wood, the workbench, the vice, jumping from the edges of the malicious chisels, soaking stickily into the crushed shavings on the floor.

Peter was unable to staunch the flow. Yet, as the blood

poured from him, the miracle happened. The appalling weeks of sadistic tension under which he had suffered (albeit with a kind of mad pleasure), the departure of Chrissie and the graceful trees which he had felled in his lunatic rage, seemed, too, to be released from their pain, to be regarding him with compassion, to be holding out their hands to him. His heart, hardened to a stone when he first looked on the chisels, now opened and beat with a softer pulse.

He rushed from the loft as once again, and with increasing brightness and ferocity, the light which had been guiding him to destruction, chased after him. He heard the harsh crying of his father's voice as he flung himself out into the acacia tree and attempted to embrace the grey, weeping bird.

The next morning the milkman, a friend of theirs, found Peter at the foot of the wooden flight of steps to the loft. He managed to get him to the house. His great strength of body had preserved him during the night. The odd thing was, there was no trace of blood on his hands or elsewhere. In fact, the milkman thought he had been sleeping off a drunken night out. Only on the open palm of his left hand lay a dead wood pigeon. The milkman kicked it aside when he picked Peter up.

Chrissie returned home in answer to a telephone call from the milkman. She found Peter lying in the great bed he had built, covered with an assortment of rugs and old coats against the autumn chill. He looked pale and shrunken and, somehow, innocent again. In that moment when he caught her to him, she knew that his father had been destroyed. He begged her to forgive him. He was openly weeping when he said, 'I've done great wrong, Chrissie. I don't deserve to be loved. I've hurt both you and the wood, the oaks and elms. But it shall be put right, I swear it. For all the agony, it wasn't the dead who conquered. And Chrissie,' he brightened, 'we're going away. As soon as you're ready, and I've attended to one or two things, we're selling up and going to Wales. I've had a marvellous offer for the property.'

'But why Wales, my dear?' She, too, was gently weeping at the joy of being home with Peter again. She wouldn't, actually, have cared if he had wanted to go to Timbuctoo.

'Because there, in some remote place, I can be finally released from him.' Chrissie nodded, knowing to whom he was referring. 'There I can be finally forgiven. I must show nature that she did not send the bird in vain. I can return to my real love.'

'Am I not that, my dear?'

'Indeed, you are. And you must never leave me again. But not my first love. That was always wood. Something horrible happened to me. All those hideous things I made have to be returned as far as possible to the form I found them in.'

'Do you mean that trolley, dear?' Chrissie had a smile. 'It's still in the kitchen, I see. Rather neglected, I'm afraid.'

'Oh, God, that trolley!' Peter groaned and turned his face from her. 'If only I'd seen what was happening to me, then, I could have stopped it all. But he was too strong for me, too full of the grave and his return, too evil with lust and desire and self-delusion. It was the chisels, his chisels, which tempted me, the desire for his kind of fame, and the awful pleasure I got from torturing the thing I loved. Oh, God, save me.'

Gently she put her hand to his cheek to soothe his agony and felt the week-old bristles. She loved him, then, entirely. 'So I am partly to blame?' she said.

'You?'

'Yes, dear. I nagged you into starting the carpentry again when I knew very well you hated it. I and he. Somehow he must have made me his agent.' They were, at that moment, like two children emerging from the depths of a dark wood, no longer afraid, at one in the safety of their love.

It was then that nature, having achieved her purpose of rescuing Peter and destroying death in resurrection, through her agents the wood pigeon, the screwdriver and the gouging of Peter's palm, allowed the ridiculous side of the situation to emerge in order to heal them completely. Or perhaps it was enough that Peter was, once more, aware of his love for Chrissie. Whatever or whoever it was, aware of the healing properties of laughter, made its protest through one of the articles of furniture he had made. An ill-shaped leg of the monstrous bed groaned and bent sideways under their weight. The whole contraption collapsed and threw them into each other's arms. They rolled in helpless laughter when they saw the idiotic angle of the bed. Peter, with a shout of joy, took her gently to him. 'Thank God,' he said, allowing his tears to mingle with hers. 'We are still young enough. I have all the time in the world to repent.'

In three months they were gone from Kent and were settled in a fairly capacious shack on the slopes of the Welsh mountains behind Aberystwyth, many acres of which Peter bought with the money he received from the sale of the house and what was left of his father's legacy. Before he left he dismantled all the furniture he had so hectically made.

With controlled anger he drove the face of each shining chisel hard against an iron bar, ruining it forever. His claw-hammer and planes, his saws and wrenches, and the vice, he buried in the great hole left by one of the oaks he had felled. On top of them he gently placed the few dried bones and shrivelled feathers of the wood pigeon, all of the bird he could find after the milkman's foot had crushed the corpse against the stable wall. As he laid the dried remains on top of the broken tools, the bones and feathers seemed to take on life, to be renewed by a gentle surfeit of bright blood. The miracle (if it were such?) made the tears leap again to his eyes. He lifted the bird on to his left hand. Slowly it took wing and was away.

When he filled in the hole it seemed to him that the tree was rising above him again in all its grace and superb leaf. Mixed with the singing of his bright spade, he thought he heard the soft murmur, 'Don't cry so, Susan; don't cry so, Susan,' of the pigeon which had given its life to save him. He knew this to be true even if he could not conceive how it could be true. The bird was now sitting in the visionary branches of the restored tree.

The last night he knelt in the loft before the pile of dismembered wood, now free of nails and screws. He prayed (to God, to Nature, he hardly knew which) to be forgiven. He wondered again how it was that when he returned to the loft to destroy all evidence of his lust, he could find no trace of the blood which had poured from his hand that night over a week ago.

In Wales, amongst the vast moor which he now owned, he began his act of contrition. Not ephemeral stuff like the Forestry Commission was planting, not pines that would mature and be cut down in thirty years time, but great oaks and beeches, ash and elm which died each winter and sprang up again in all their glory the following spring. Eventually the great trees populated and cast their summer shade over the bare mountainside. They formed a shield of living wood. Peter had erected a natural barrier of green life against the death and possible return of his father. He was taking no chances.

No one but Chrissie ever understood why he never sold any of his wood or allowed anyone to cut down a tree. As he grew into an old man, and the trees sheltered him and Chrissie even more, he came to be regarded as a local eccentric. The other thing Chrissie never fully understood, and was wise enough not to ask about – Peter would never allow a wood pigeon to be shot over any of his land.

VII

In The Box

Frank Baker

You realize that every question put to you must be answered truthfully, quietly, and – most important – precisely. No fancy words. Few adjectives. If possible let your answers be 'yes' or 'no'. Nothing more. For here, in the box, you are only a cipher. And yet you are also unique. And this fact will come piercing as an arrow to you, driving to heart and head and reminding you that you are alone. Alone in a way you never have been before. And you will realize also that there is no way of escape. Time ceases to exist. You could be here forever. Clocks may tick; but they have no meaning in court.

Nobody helps you. You look around, guardedly, perhaps through half closed eyelids. You are aware of a smudge of many faces. Jury, wigged counsels, police, anonymous minute strangers in a small gallery, and – the Judge. You are becoming interred into a kind of floodlit darkness. You know that you must strive to avoid catching anybody's eyes, especially the Judge's, should he address you. (And you never know when this might happen.) Direct visual encounter is a danger; and it is this, you will find, that everybody else in court desires – to look straight into your eyes. Because in your eyes truth will be naked. So look down, if it seems natural, or sideways. You will try to stand at ease after you have sworn the 'whole truth.'

'The whole truth.' This I had sworn. I said just now that you must answer every question truthfully. Yes. But truth can be positive and negative. What you state and what you withhold. And what you do not say is what they all want to know.

Counsel for the Prosecution is addressing me; I hear him now.

'Mr Wilburn, you say that on the night of November the 1st you arrived at the Land's End Hotel after a long drive from your home in London?'

My answer: 'Yes, Sir.' (Ridiculously, one hopes the 'Sir' will help.)

'Accompanied by a young lady, Sheila Foster, who asked you for a lift somewhere near Okehampton.'

To this, I merely nod in assent. It has all been gone over so many times before.

'You dined together, then went fairly early to bed?'

'Yes.' (I decide occasionally to drop the 'Sir'. One has to beware of obsequiousness. It tends to suspicion from the jury.)

A pause. I am suddenly aware of one member of the jury, a fat middle-aged woman, staring intently at me, as though she knew me. I shift my eyes slightly upwards where all seems strangely dark.

'And this unfortunate girl's bedroom was next to yours.'

Again, I murmur, 'Yes ...' leaving the 'Sir' hanging in the air.

Suddenly, his manner changes. He is sharper. That is one of their tricks to catch you. From sweet to sour, for no apparent reason.

'You stated that you could not sleep well.'

A pause, which is like eternity. Again, I restrain my words. 'That is so.'

'May I ask – and please take your time, Mr Wilburn – did you get out of bed?'

The wearing-down process is beginning. I do take my time. And finally: 'Yes. For an obvious reason.'

A mistake. I am aware of the smallest ripple of laughter from the jury-box.

'An obvious reason. Could you be more precise?'

A new voice sounds, from above and beyond me. It seems to be far away, on another plane. 'Mr Hancock, I imagine the members of the jury know the reason.'

It is the Judge who has spoken, almost charitably, yet dispassionate. But Prosecution will not let it pass.

'M'Lud, if I may say so, there could be many reasons for which one leaves one's bed on a wild winter night. An important point turns on the answer to my question.'

'Very good, Mr Hancock. Proceed.'

Counsel does proceed. Would I be good enough to tell my Lord and the jury why I left my bed?

Crucial question, and one I know that I must answer convincingly. And to be too slow is to tremble on the brink of the pit Prosecution is digging for me. I curse myself for using the phrase 'obvious reason'. And this leads to a fatal decision.

'In order to get some sleeping tablets from my bag, which was the other side of the room.'

Prosecution smiles. Almost purring, he turns to the jury.

'An obvious reason.' He lets this sink in. Then, back to me, swift as a hawk. 'You had not, as is your custom, placed the tablets by the side of the bed?'

'As is your custom.' How has he assumed that? Have I mentioned it in an earlier statement? I begin to sweat now. And the one word 'No' is forced out from me.

Why am I here? Is it customary to call the accused person into the witness-box? And what is the charge? The murder of the girl who hitched a lift on that long drive westwards? Or – my wife? Or – both? No. There can only be one charge. The girl.

My mind begins to flounder. I am like a bit of wreckwood, tossed about in the sea. I shall not know how to answer the next question. Restrain, restrain – I tell myself. Say as little as possible. Leave it to your Defence Counsel. It is his business to clear you.

'Mr Wilburn, having found your essential sedatives, what did you do next?'

How cleverly he reduces me, with the word 'essential'. An answer chokes in me. My mouth is dry. And yet it is all so simple. Merely to say that I took a glass of water, swallowed the Mogadon, and returned to bed. But the answer will not come. Or, when it does come, it falls too late from my lips, and the hesitations betray me.

' ... Naturally ... I ... searched in ... my bag ... for ... for ...

for ... and the next thing I did was ...'

Clack-clack from Prosecution. 'I suggest to you, Mr Wilburn, that the tablets were already by your bed. And that you left your bed, put on some clothes, and left the room, having heard the sound of a door opening, next to your room.'

The dreamy faraway voice sounds. The Voice that seems to have no interest in these mundane proceedings. The casual voice of the Judge, to whom murder is a commonplace.

'Be good enough, Mr Hancock, to ask the witness a straight question. You are not here to "suggest".'

'Your pardon, M'Lud. Mr Wilburn, I will put it precisely.' And then, suddenly, crackshot: 'Did you leave your room?' Spoken like one word.

The faces in the jury-box merge into one Daumier-like gargoyle: grinning, twitching, snarling, ogling. And still I have not answered. The question is repeated.

'Mr Wilburn ...' and now he speaks gently, as though to lull me. 'Mr Wilburn, I am asking you a simple question. Having heard the door of the adjoining room open, and footsteps along the corridor – the footsteps of the unfortunate young person you had picked up on the road – did you leave your room, go downstairs to reception, and leave the hotel?'

Had I left my room? In the few seconds in which I consider the answer, a tidal wave of questions floods over me. The shattering of my whole life splinters me. My dying wife's accusing eyes as I tell her how much she means to me, or how little. The daily, deadly little deeds of deceit. Fraud, envy, malice. Failure to love. Pretence – always pretence. The slow build-up of a modest fortune. Hoarding of money I have no need for. Indolence. Impotence. Insensibility. Like little hogs snuffling for truffles, they sniff at me and find me as empty as spectacles without lenses. This man, questioning me, drills right through me. My flesh falls away. I am nothing but stripped bones.

Had I left my room?

Crazily I reply: 'No.' And then, with sudden force, like a desperate man who reaches out for a spar of wreckwood as the sea heaves him back and away: 'No. I did not leave my room.'

(The rapid pulling on of trousers over my pyjamas. Jacket, scarf, and topcoat. Quiet opening of the door. The measured walk down the long softly-carpeted corridor. The rapid beating of the heart as the footsteps keep slow pace. The reception desk. The porter still in his office, half asleep. A clock showing eleven-thirty. The murmur of my own voice, to which the porter makes no response, 'Just want a little air.' And then – out to the wind shoring up from the warm west. Exhilaration. Thank God for the warm west ...)

A voice sounds, seemingly from another world. 'And so, Mr Wilburn, you did not leave your room.'

'*No.*' The word flays me as I hear it again now.

'And yet, we have evidence that somebody did leave the hotel, at about eleven-thirty, only a few minutes after Sheila Foster had also left.'

This is not a question. It calls for no answer. I look down to my Defence Counsel. But he is seated, his face buried in his hands, his long legs stretched out. Why doesn't he get up and protest? He is my Angel. Why can't he come to my rescue?

I hear myself shouting. And in the shout the whole Court shivers and shrinks. I am alone here, in the box, with people small as insects in a vast mausoleum.

'*I tell you, I did not leave my room.*'

(As the idiotic lie barks from me I stand again on the great stacks of granite at Land's End. And there she is, the girl who hitched a lift on the endless drive from London to Bolerium. The girl I had cried out for, to restore my confidence. Waiting for a lift, and never knowing that she must give one. A lost waif with a battered suitcase. Going nowhere, only waiting for a lift. I am old enough to be her father. But if I could get her to bed ... to prove myself. And she needs comfort. Now, there she stands, high above the sea, her mouth wide open, her fresh youth drawing in the sweet heather-ridden air. Why has she come out here? Why wouldn't she come to my bed? What does she want from life? Is it something you can give her?)

Like a trumpet, a voice sounds.

'You declare that you did not leave your room. That you

did not leave the hotel. And yet we have clear evidence that ...'

Again, the other voice, a weary voice with a controlled sigh of compassion in it.

'Mr Hancock, I must ask you not to submit the witness to ...'

But Mr Hancock is reckless now, and will not give way to the Judge. 'M'Lud, if I may be allowed to proceed. It has clearly been established that Sheila Foster left the hotel at about eleven-twenty. That the witness was seen going out, very soon afterwards. And that he returned, twenty minutes later, in a distraught condition. Will the members of the jury look at this individual in the witness-box and ask themselves ...'

In the box, slowly it dawns upon you that further speech is useless. The eyes you seeked to avoid from these insects are now glinting at you, till they become one great burning eye, searing you. The court is lost in the swirling wind and mist of Land's End. The wind rises with a howl. The girl you wanted, who would not share a room with you, is now in your arms. In the wind, in the mist, why not? You try her gently at first. You intend to comfort. But she screams. 'No ... No ... ' Why does she scream? What did she expect when she asked for a lift? Why doesn't she let you lead her back to your room, and be civilized about it? Does she think you are trying to rape her?

You begin to knock. Looking at your curved knuckles you see them red and raw, knocking on the desk of the box. Or is it a desk?

And then, suddenly, a sad, resigned voice. 'I have no more questions, M'Lud.'

Where is my Angel? Has he no questions to ask?

No. He sits back, head lowered. Has he presented your case, or is it lost? Again, you hear the Voice, a gurgle of meaningless words.

'Ladies and Gentlemen of the Jury, in considering this case do not allow yourselves to think of anything but the condition of the unfortunate girl, Sheila Foster, whose dead and sexually mutilated body was found some fifteen feet below in a ...'

... And still you knock, until your knuckles are bleeding. Again you cry, words that nobody hears: 'I never left my room.'

Whatever he said, Defence has not been able to establish a case for you. The summing-up swings relentlessly in one direction. Years go by as you wait. Your whole little life canters mockingly before you.

And then, after the court has adjourned and the jury returned, one word slithers from one mouth. 'Guilty.'

It is strange, the eroding consolation there is in the truth. Guilty. But of course. Why was all this tedious examination necessary? You could have pleaded that and saved a lot of insects a lot of trouble. Guilty. In the word, I hear now not the slash and smash of the sea against the gigantic granite stacks of Bolerium; I hear only the gentle sliding of waves upon the gentler sands. In the box, from which there is no escape, there lies a kind of peace. The Judge is giving sentence. I think he will go on till Doomsday. And in the whole court an antidote of sympathy swells out. It is all so long ago. So long, so long, so long ago. And Ada, poor Ada, my wife, who could never respond; who made me impotent. Trying to be 'good'. No children. It was better to finish her, for she had no love either for me, or for herself. At least my hands were strong.

I leave her, dead on the bed where there had been no consummation. And I leave behind me the years of work in the Underwriting Room, the wide clean desk, the slips for me to sign day by day. All those years, so absurd, nothing accomplished. Only my scrawled initials on slips of paper, insuring this craft and that craft.

I live again the long drive down, and see the girl with the suitcase, waiting, her hand upraised. A body made for love. (I hear the word 'Guilty' again, but so quietly, it is like a bell-buoy in a summer dawn). 'She is sent to me,' I say. And so she was, for an end I could not foresee. I would take that young body and do what I liked with it. Oh, not to be cruel! Oh no! But to bring her to life, to bring both of us to life. For that is what she wanted. Some punk had let her down. And she is cold, wretched. There is nothing before her. She does not care where I take her. She revels only in the warmth of the car. All of those miles from the house in London where Ada lay dead, she is half asleep, sometimes murmuring. My left hand wanders over her sprawled, open thighs, to the centre of her being. She stirs a little; but no resistance. I could have stopped then and ... but no, I wanted civilized comfort for her. So on and on I drove, smooth as a swift. The road catches me, the empty winter road, until we are across Tamar and into Cornwall. A molten sun blinds me. It blinds me now. What tense do I speak in, or am I even speaking? The sun drops down blood-red into a gathering shroud of mist. Truro. Penzance. On and on. Where can I stop? Only at the end.

Land's End. Bolerium, as the ancients called it, where I spent a holiday with Ada a quarter of a century ago. But what is a quarter of a century now?

At last, almost on the edge of the cliff, the car stops. Darkness now, and that old familiar roar of the wind wooing the sea. Longships stands erect under a half-moon. It is warm and sticky, the earth is sweating, the very air drenched with desire, as I am – drenched with sweat and a surging strength rising in me as I anticipate the night.

She wakes, the girl I picked up.

'We'll stay the night here. What do you say?'

Yes. What else can she say? But she will not share a room with me, stupid little bitch. For had she done so ... oh God, I wish I could forget that timid refusal. So – separate rooms; and reception assuming she is my daughter. Too late for dinner. Sandwiches and drinks sent up to our rooms. She stands by her door. 'Thank you so much. You've been so kind. In the morning ...'

How can I sleep, with her next door? Here, in the box, I reflect on it all. I tap on the wood of the box. Nobody hears. Perhaps my knuckles are too weak. Where is the court? Is it still sitting? Or is some other poor devil standing where I ...

Where I stand? No. I am not standing. I tap again, feebly. I feel an impotent rebellion rising in me, as I felt when I grasped her body and she fell from me and tumbled over the cliff. They must let me leave the box.

But I cannot. My tapping is useless. There is no escape. You have to accept. Once you're in the box you're well in it, and that is as certain as sunrise, even when you don't see it rise.

Oh this wood – it is hard, so hard. I hear the Judge again. 'Be good enough Mr Hancock to ask the witness a straight question. You are not here to suggest.'

A straight question.

'James Wilburn, are you guilty?'

But this is not the usual procedure of the court. Nonetheless, there is only one answer.

'Yes, my Lord. I am guilty, of more than you know.'

Oh, this box – why can't I move? I'm so tired of lying here, swathed like a mummy. A mummy! That's a good one. Poor Ada, she never heard the word spoken to her. I'm so sick of lying here. And what is that muted, emasculated music from an electric organ? *I know that my Redeemer liveth.* Do I know? Not if it sounds like that. No. My Redeemer is dead; and my Angel, my Defence has slunk away out of the case. There is only the Judge.

I knock again. Bones on wood. No response. I hear footsteps, very slow footsteps. Is it people filing into court? Or filing out? Not many people, I think. Perhaps twelve. It is all so long ago ...

A dreary voice comes to me, spoken through a veil of self-deceit.

'I am the Resurrection and the Life ...'

No. No. I must break out of this damned box. They have not treated me fairly. None of them, all now so quiet, shuffling their knees down, as the dreary voice goes on.

I attempt to knock again; but my hand will not move.

What is that new sound? A kind of trickling – but that isn't right. It is the sound of curtains being slowly drawn aside.

My Lord, thank you for movement. I feel the box sliding away, like cruising downhill with the engine off. Coming to rest at the Land's End Hotel.

Slide ... slide ... slide ...

'Mr Wilburn, welcome.'

Whoever speaks, it is comforting. But I wish I could have had her that night. The bed could have warmed us both. We could have had so rich a night. But now it is all over. If only we could have gone together, if only I could have fallen over the cliff with her. I never meant to kill Ada. I never meant to ... all the bad things I have done ...

I will speak somehow. 'My Lord, if I could be allowed to say something in my defence.'

'Pray, proceed, Mr Wilburn.'

'Why hammer nails into the box?'

But the curtains have come together again now and I am on the other side. I realize that I must answer every question truthfully, quietly, and precisely. Yet, I am unique. And I am alone. I have never known before what loneliness is.

'Mr Wilburn, your case will be considered in due course. Millions have come here before you. Millions will come after you. Mr Wilburn, do not fuss. Your time in the box is ended.'

VIII

The Basket Chair

Winston Graham

(i)

Whiteleaf had his first coronary when he was staying with his niece Agnes and her husband Roy Paynter. He came through it, as of course he fully expected he would. When a healthy man is struck down with a near fatal blow it is as if he has walked into a brick wall in the dark; he is brought up starkly against the realisation of his own mortality, and there is nothing to cushion the psychological shock. But Julian Whiteleaf had lived so closely with his own mortality for so long that a heart attack was just another obstacle to be carefully surmounted and added to his list of battle scars. No doubt this attitude of mind had helped him to stay alive when probability was not on his side.

But this was a nasty business, so painful and so disabling. It was hospital for three weeks and then it would be another four at least in Agnes's house before he was well enough to go home. The doctor had been a little reluctant to let him out of hospital, but Whiteleaf badly wanted to leave and Agnes had had some training as a nurse and said she could manage, as Roy was out all day. She was a highly efficient woman.

Although she was his only surviving relative Whiteleaf had never really cared for Agnes. She was a childless, stocky, formidable woman of forty, who made ends meet on Roy's inadequate salary and found time and money for endless good works. Yet whether it was the Red Cross or the Women's Institute or the Homebound Club, every good deed was performed with the same grim patient efficiency so that joy was noticeably lacking from the occasion. Far better,

Whiteleaf thought – and had sometimes said – if she took a paid job of her own to supplement the family income; but this advice was not appreciated.

So in some ways he would have been happy enough to stay another week or so in hospital; but as he had opted out of the Health Service some time ago it saved a great deal of money to leave, and anyway he rather thought Agnes liked making the effort to prove her devotion.

Another four weeks with Agnes, mainly in bed, was a daunting prospect. But the time would pass. Whiteleaf was a great reader, and Agnes brought a portable radio up to his bedroom. He would have time to ruminate, time to rest. At sixty-five one becomes philosophical.

He had had an interesting life, and it bore looking back on. Born above a small bookshop in Bloomsbury, he had been vaguely literary from an early age but his talents had lain in the unprofitable fields for which Bloomsbury in the thirties offered so much scope. Apart from helping in his father's bookshop, he had worked on two Fabian magazines, then had been assistant editor on a Theosophist newspaper which shortly folded up; he had reviewed and done freelance work, had dabbled in Spiritualism and then become secretary to the Society for Psychoneural Research. Here he met Mrs Melanie Buxton who financed the society, and had become her lover.

At this stage the war had come and he had found himself a reluctant soldier entering a world which had almost no physical or psychological resemblance to the ingrown, rather intense, fringe-intellectual world he had inhabited before. For a while the fresh air and the hard life did him good. He strengthened and broadened and mellowed under it. But in 1943 he was invalided out, having been twice seriously wounded in the desert and having contracted asthma and a kidney complaint from which he would suffer for the rest of his life.

To his surprise he found himself a rich man. Mrs Melanie Buxton, who was twenty years older than he was, had just died, and she left the bulk of her personal fortune – about £200,000 – to Julian Whiteleaf, 'to help him continue in the paths of research to which we are both devoted'.

Whiteleaf sold the bookshop, which he had also just inherited, and at forty years of age settled down to the existence of a quiet, ailing, dilettante. He never went back to live in Bloomsbury but bought himself a pleasant service flat in Hurlingham and never moved again. There was no one to oversee his interpretation of Mrs Buxton's will, but to fulfil the spirit of the bequest he kept the society in being with a tiny office and a secretary and continued to review books and write articles on paranormal phenomena. So, gradually, he had become something of an authority. Once or twice he helped to conduct inquiries into so-called haunted houses. He continued to dabble in Theosophy. He was known as a fair-minded commentator on the spiritualist scene. He was neither a committed believer nor a scoffing sceptic. Editors of national newspapers, confronted with an unusual book which did not quite fit into any of the recognised slots, would say: 'Oh, send it to Whiteleaf; see what he makes of it.'

He never married. His experiences with Mrs Buxton had satisfied him, and his ill-health after the war was a sufficient disincentive to extreme physical effort.

He joined a good London club and had many friendly acquaintances there or among those with interests like his own; but he had no real friends. He did not feel the lack of them. He looked at life through books. He was a precise, quiet man, sandy and rather small, who spoke without moving his lips. He lived very much within his income and never gave money away, except £20 to his niece each Christmas.

His visits to her were annual and largely a duty. She was the daughter of his sister who had died in the fifties, and blood, he supposed, etc ... but it was really rather an effort. He would, he knew, have made an excuse to stop the visits before this, had it not been for her husband Roy, who had a responsible but dead-end and underpaid job on the railways, and who, apart from being a nice inoffensive chap for whom Whiteleaf felt some sympathy at having married Agnes, also appealed to the other interest in Whiteleaf's life, which was the steam-engine.

This was the topic of conversation four nights out of the

seven that Whiteleaf usually came to spend with them, especially when Agnes was out on some charitable mission; and sometimes at the week-end the two men would go to the railway museum, which was only a few miles away, and study the old locomotives and compare notes. It was a bond. And when he was dangerously ill two years ago after a gall-bladder operation, Roy had come up to London each week-end to see him and had brought up old catalogues and lists of engines from the days of steam, which he had been able to borrow from the local files.

Now that Whiteleaf was convalescing in their house and for a lengthy period, he felt he should pay them something for his keep, and he offered them £5 a week which Agnes accepted – grudgingly, he thought. But it would be a considerable help to them, he well knew, and not to be sniffed at, his weekly cheque. Agnes spent no more time on him than she would have done on her unpaid good works. The doctor called daily and Agnes took his blood pressure night and morning when she gave him his pills. And a starvation diet. His £5 was all profit.

Convalescence is a strange experience. Whiteleaf was used to it, but 'every time', he wrote in his diary a couple of days after he came back from hospital, 'it presents a new face. It is as if the mind during serious illness concentrates all its energies on survival; but once the crisis is past it relaxes. It even relaxes its normal vigilance and controls – so that strange fancies, wayward concepts, take a hold that in normal times of health they would never begin to do. Nerves are on edge, imagination gets loose, temper frays as if one were a child again. Why snap at Agnes over the fire in my room? She so obviously is doing her best. Why allow oneself to think so much about the basket chair?'

Whiteleaf's diary was the one thing he had kept to all his life. Very often he wrote in it thoughts which later were useful to him when reviewing books or writing articles. He had been glad to get back to it when the doctor's prohibition was removed, and to fill in the empty days. He had always done this after his operations, even calling on the nurses to help him. This time happily there had been no unconsciousness, only great pain and then forced immobility.

'Of course,' he wrote two days after that, 'one wonders how far all paranormal phenomena is explained in this way. And in this context, what does "explained" mean? "Imagination gets loose", I see I wrote overleaf. But how do we separate illusion from reality? We define reality as something which because it is apprehended by the majority of men is therefore assumed to exist. But does consensus of opinion necessarily prove the *positive* of any theory of reality? Still less therefore can it disprove the negative. Galileo believed that the earth moved round the sun. His was the scientific eye, perceiving what others could not see. May not the psychic eye perceive another area of truth at present hidden from the rest of us?'

'Is something worrying you, Uncle?' Roy asked that evening when he was sitting with him after supper.

'No. Why?'

'You kept staring at the fireplace as if something didn't please you.'

'Not at all. Nothing is worrying me. But in fact I was looking at that chair on the other side beside the lamp.'

'That one? What about it?'

'It's new, isn't it? I mean new to you? Since my last visit.'

'We've had it about a year. Agnes bought it at a sale. It's a bit of a rickety old thing but it's very comfortable. You'll be able to try it in another week or so.'

'It looks seventy or eighty years old to me.'

'Maybe. But it's *strong*. The frame's strong. Like iron. It's quite heavy to lift. I think Agnes paid a pound for it. About this film ...'

They returned to discussing *La Bête Humaine*, which Whiteleaf had seen thirty years ago and considered the best film about railways ever made. Roy had never seen it and wanted to. There were copies in France, and being in railways he might be able to pull a string or two. He also knew the proprietor of the local cinema who, between alternate bingo nights, was always willing to risk a bit of something way-out. He preferred sex or horror films, but if the French film were offered to him to show for a couple of nights without rental charge he would certainly agree to show it.

But it would cost money to bring it over and to put it on. It was no good Roy trying to do anything unless he knew Uncle Julian would bear the cost. Uncle Julian was doubtful, discouraging: he'd want to know a lot more about what he was letting himself in for before he even considered it. They discussed it for a long time and came as near an argument as they ever got, Roy pressing and Whiteleaf hedging away.

After Roy had gone Agnes came in and settled him down for the night. It was diuretic pills in the morning and potassium pills at night, and she gave him these now and saw his inhaler was within reach, threw some slack coal on the fire, which kept it in most of the night but almost extinguished it as a provider of heat, and then stood by the bed, square and uncompromising, and asked him if he wanted anything more.

He said no and she kissed his forehead perfunctorily and left. It was eleven o'clock. He read for a few minutes and then put out the light and composed himself for sleep. The room and the house were very quiet. Roy and Agnes were separated from him by the bathroom and the box room and their movements could not be heard. In the distance a diesel train hooted. It was a lonely sound.

Then the basket chair creaked as if someone had just sat down in it.

(ii)
'I think,' said Dr Abrahams, 'you might have stayed in another week. Are you moving about too much?'

'No. Only once or twice a day, with my niece's help, just as you advised.'

'He never has need to stir a finger otherwise,' said Agnes uncompromisingly.

'Well, the electrocardiograms are satisfactory. But why aren't you sleeping?'

'I do well enough when I get off, but it takes an hour or two to – compose myself.'

'He sleeps in the afternoon,' Agnes said. 'I expect that takes the edge off. I can *never* sleep at night if I have a nap after lunch.'

'The breathing all right?'

'No worse than usual. I always need the inhaler a few times.'

After the doctor had gone, Agnes came back and found Whiteleaf writing in his diary.

'You shouldn't do that,' she said. 'It tires you. Dr Abrahams was asking me if you were worried about something. I said not so far as I know.'

'Not so far as I know either. Tell me, Agnes, about that basket chair. Roy says you bought it in a sale.'

Agnes looked rather peculiar. 'Yes. Why? What's wrong with it?'

'Nothing at all. But what sale?'

'Oh, it was that big house about a mile out of Swindon. D'you remember it? No, you won't, I don't expect.'

'D'you mean Furze Hall?'

'No. Beyond that. There was a Miss Covent lived there, all by herself with only one servant. It had thirty-four rooms. Fantastic. She was eighty when she died.'

'What made you go?'

'Oh, it was advertised. Carol Elliot wanted a few things – you know, from down the road – so I went with her. It was an awful old place; she'd let it go to ruin, this Miss Covent: all the roofs leaked, I should think; it's being pulled down. Most of the furniture was junk but it went very cheap. I paid a pound for the chair and ten bob for that bookcase in the hall and two pounds for four kitchen mats and –'

Agnes went on about her bargains and then switched to some other subject, which Whiteleaf ignored.

'Did you know anything about it?' he asked presently. 'About the house where you bought those things?'

'The Covents' place? Well, of course, I'd never been in before. Hardly anyone had. It was like something out of Boris Karloff, I can tell you. The old lady must have been bats living there alone. There was some story Carol Elliot was telling me about it but I didn't pay much attention.'

'Ask her sometime.'

'Carol? Yes, I'll ask her. But why?'

'I'm interested in old places. You know my interests.'

'Well, I never heard it was *haunted*, if that's what you mean. Don't you like the chair? I can take it out.'

'No, leave it where it is. I like old things.'

'Well, it's comfy, I can tell you that. I always enjoy sitting in it when I come to see you last thing.'

When she had gone Whiteleaf continued in his diary: 'Recorded and authenticated "possession" of small items of furniture is relatively rare and has no reliable weight of testimony behind it such as the "possession" of houses has. The poltergeist one accepts, because one has to accept it. Beyond that there is only reasonable cause to believe and reasonable cause to doubt. In the case of a chair ... ' He wrote no more that evening.

The following day he began a new entry. 'Is this the hallucination of illness or the clearer perception of convalescence? It is certainly a very peculiar shape. That high rounded back. It is a half-way style, reminiscent of one of the old hooded hall chairs of the 18th century. Why does someone or something appear to sit in it every night when I am trying to go to sleep? And am I right in supposing sometimes that I can hear breathing and footsteps? Odd that in all these years of interest and study this should be the first possibly psychic event that has ever happened to me ...'

The next evening Agnes said: 'I saw Carol today. It is a funny story about the Covents. Of course, she's lived here all her life and we've only been here ten years. She says it was before her time but her mother often spoke of it.'

'Spoke of what?' Whiteleaf asked.

'Well, it's not a very nice story, Uncle. It won't upset you to talk about it?'

'I'm not made of cotton wool,' he said impatiently. 'In any case, how can something that presumably happened years ago have any effect? I'm allowed to read the daily papers, aren't I?'

'Yes, well, yes ... ' Agnes plucked at her lip. 'Well, Carol says they were a young married couple, the Covents, during World War One. He was in the Battle of the Somme and was blown up and hideously disfigured. Apparently spent a couple of years in hospital and then they let him out. I suppose plastic surgery wasn't much help in those days ...'

'No, it was in an experimental stage.'

'So they hadn't done him any good. He was still terrible to look at, and when he came home he never went out of the house but used to sit by the fire all day reading and thinking. His wife used to go out and do all the shopping, etc., Carol's mother says, and that way she met another man and had an affair with him. Somehow or other Captain Covent discovered this and it must have turned his brain because she suddenly stopped going shopping and everyone thought they had gone away ...'

Whiteleaf felt his heart give a slight excited lurch. 'Interesting.'

'After a few weeks someone got suspicious and they broke into the house and there they were, both dead, one on either side of the empty fireplace. Apparently he'd tied her to a chair and then sat down opposite her and watched her starve to death. Then he cut his own throat. That's what the doctors said. It was a big sensation in the twenties.'

'Very interesting,' said Whiteleaf.

'Well, horrible I say. They hadn't any children so the property came to his eldest sister and she took it over and lived there until last year. I tell you the house would have given me the creeps without any funny stories.'

Silence fell and the door downstairs banged.

'That's Roy,' said Agnes. 'I'll get him to shift that chair tonight, just so that it won't worry you.'

'Not at all,' said Whiteleaf. 'Leave it just where it is.'

Agnes shivered. 'Don't tell Roy. He's superstitious about these things.'

Whiteleaf shifted himself up the bed. 'D'you realise I remember the First World War?'

'Do you, Uncle? Yes, I suppose you do. But you'd be very young.'

'I well remember celebrating the Armistice. I was thirteen at the time. It never occurred to me then that I should have to fight in another war myself.'

When she had gone downstairs to get Roy his tea, Whiteleaf wrote just one sentence in his diary. 'I wonder if this chair, this basket chair, was the one Captain Covent sat in? Or was it hers?'

(iii)
That night, although he was still not sure about the breathing, he was quite certain about the footsteps. The creaking of the chair as someone sat in it began about ten minutes or so after he was left alone and went on for a little while with faint furtive creaks. They were very faint but very distinct as someone stirred in the chair. Then also quite distinctly there was the soft pad of footsteps, about six or seven, moving away from the chair towards the door. They did not reach the door. They stopped half-way and were heard no more. Presently the creaking died away.

It is surprising what tension is generated by the supernatural. One can write about it. One can attend spiritualist séances. One can even visit haunted houses and still remain detached, scientific, aloof. But in a silent bedroom, entirely alone, with only this wayward wandering spirit for company, Julian Whiteleaf felt himself screwing up to meet some crisis that he greatly feared but could not imagine. It was clearly not doing his health much good or aiding his recovery. The whole thing was strikingly interesting; but he would have to take care, to take great care, to find some means of rationalising this experience so that he could regain his detachment. Only his diary helped.

'Supposing,' he wrote, 'that I am *not* the victim of a sick man's hallucination and that for some reason I have become clairaudient. (The "some reason" could well be the rare combination of my hypersensitive perceptions during convalescence and the presence of a chair with such an evil aura, amounting to "possession".) Supposing that, then is there any resolution or solution of the situation in which I find myself? Is there any *progress* in this nightly occurrence?

there a likelihood that I may become clairvoyant too? (And in the circumstances would I wish to be? Hardly!) Why are there only six or seven steps, and why do they always move towards the door?'

That night there were exactly the same number of steps but they were quite audible now, a soft firm foot-fall, measured but fading at the usual spot.

Whiteleaf never kept his light on, but Agnes had lent him her electric clock, which had an illuminated face, so that when one's eyes were accustomed to the dark one could just see about the room. And tonight a pale blue flame was flickering in the fire, so this helped. But sitting up in bed, Whiteleaf wished there had been no such fire, for the flame conjured up movements about the old chair. He thought: insanity is not evil, yet it so often wears the same guise. Covent must have been insane, driven insane by his own mutilated face rather than by jealousy of his wife. Only an insane man could tie a woman to a chair and watch her starve to death. I must examine that chair more closely. There may even be signs of where the rope has frayed the frame.

It was four o'clock in the morning before he fell asleep.

(iv)
Dr Abrahams said to Agnes: 'Your uncle is not making the progress that I'd hoped for. His blood pressure is up a little and his breathing is not too satisfactory. If this goes on we'll get him back in hospital.'

'It's just as you like,' said Agnes. 'I always help him when he gets out of bed, and we're careful he doesn't overdo it. I keep the fire going all day and night to help his asthma.'

'Of course he uses that inhaler too much: I've told him to go easy on it, but it would be unwise to take it away; he has come to depend on it. One is between the devil and the deep sea.'

'I'll watch him,' said Agnes. 'But he *is* difficult. Strong minded. He'd fight before he went back to hospital.'

'That's what I'm afraid of,' said Abrahams.

While they were downstairs talking, Whiteleaf was up and examining the chair, as he had done once before when left to himself. As Roy had said, it was a strangely heavy chair for one made principally of cane. The framework was of a thin rounded wood like bamboo but enormously hard. You couldn't make any indentation in it with a fruit knife. There were a number of stains on the seat under the cushion: they could have been bloodstains: impossible without forensic equipment to tell. Whiteleaf had never sat in the chair and did not want to do so now. He felt he might have been sitting on something that should not be there. Only Agnes sat on it, in the evenings, and he had been tempted more than once to ask her not to.

He hastily climbed back into bed as he heard her feet on the stairs.

Later he wrote: 'I get the feeling that someone or something is trying to escape. To escape from the bondage of the chair. (Not surprising, perhaps, in view of its history!) But something more than just that – otherwise why the steps? It's as if the body rotted away long ago but the spirit is still attached to the scene of its suffering and still striving to get away. The footsteps always move towards the door. If they ever reached the door, would Something go out? This I could accept more readily were this the actual room in which the tragedy took place. Yet perhaps in the room in which this *did* happen, there *were* only eight steps from chair to door. Perhaps after the tragedy the chair was not moved for years and this "possession", this spirit, became bound for ever to a routine of "escape" each night. Even so it does *not* escape: it repeats for ever the ghastly ritual. Could it now in this new situation really escape for ever if the footsteps could reach *this* door? How to encourage them?'

It was the following day that he had the idea. Agnes, with her passion for cleanliness, was scouring his room as she did every day, and when she moved the basket chair to vacuum under it he suddenly called to her not to put it back.

Frowning she switched off the vacuum and listened.

'Don't put the chair back there. Put it – put it just by the dressing-table, just to the left of the dressing-table. I think I fancy it over there.'

She did not move. 'What's the matter, Uncle? Doesn't the furniture suit you? I do my best, you know.'

'You do very well,' he said. 'I'm not complaining, but if you move the chair by the dressing-table it will give me a better view of the fire.'

She stared. 'I don't see how it can. The fire ... ' She stopped and shrugged. 'Oh, well, it makes no difference to me. If that's your fancy. *Where* d'you want it?'

'Over there. A bit further. That's a good place for it there, I think.'

'D'you want me to move this other chair over? Make more room for the commode.'

'Er – no. No, just leave that. Thank you, Agnes.' He began to say something more but she had switched on the vacuum again.

He didn't really mind because he was counting the steps. At the most the chair was now seven from the door.

'An experiment,' he wrote in his diary. 'Possibly nothing will come of it. Possibly shall have interfered with the "possession" altogether. Or possibly the footsteps will reach the door and something will *go out*.'

He spent the rest of the day quietly reading an old book on the Great Western Railway which Roy had brought him. This, he thought, was one of the sagas of our time. The wonderful Castle locomotives that set up records seventy years ago which have never been broken. The 4-4-0's that preceded them. The Cities and the Kings ... He wished he could concentrate. He wished, perhaps, that he had agreed to pay the expense of having that old film over, even though it dealt with French railways and French engines. They were indeed majestic in their own right. The great snorting locomotives of the Train Bleu, of the Orient Express, with their strange pulsating beat even when they are at rest ... He wished he could concentrate.

Roy was out that evening at a social affair, Masonic or Rotary or something, so he did not see him. Agnes came up as usual, and, in spite of its uncustomary position, she sat in the basket chair. It was on the tip of his tongue to ask her not to; but again he refrained, partly because he was afraid of her uncomprehending stare, with its half implication that Uncle must be going a bit peculiar, and partly because her having been in the chair had not affected the manifestation on earlier nights.

She stayed longer than normal, talking about some work she was doing for refugees, and he listened impatiently, longing for her to be gone. She stayed in fact until Roy came in, by which time it was nearly midnight; then she gave the fire an unsympathetic poke, thumped his pillow, saw that he had enough water for the night, gave him her perfunctory kiss and was gone.

Roy had come straight upstairs, and the house soon settled. Whiteleaf's heart was thumping. To try to ease it, he began to compose the article he would write for one of the psychic papers on his experiences with a basket chair. One of the psychic papers? But possibly *The Guardian* would print it, or even *The Times*. It all depended upon the end, upon the resolution. It all depended on what happened tonight. In a way it was a triumph, that a man so involved as he had been all his life in paranormal phenomena, should at this late stage *experience* it in the most personal way. To steady himself, he tried to look on it as if it had already happened. He was recounting the most exciting moment of his life. The trouble was it wasn't over yet; he was in the middle of it; and the final experience, if there was one, was yet to come.

The fire was burning a little brighter tonight; Agnes had forgotten to bring up as much slack as usual, and this, with the help of the clock, gave adequate light – though dim. He could see all but the corners of the room. The chair in its new position was not so clearly outlined as it had been by the fire: it looked taller, still more hump-backed, like a man without a head. It cast a faint shadow on the wall behind that did not look quite its own.

The creaking was late coming tonight. He had thought it might not come at all. Always it began with a fairly definite over-all creaking such as would occur when Mrs Covent first sat in it. Then it would be silent, except for the faint creaks that broke out whenever she moved. There was no sign of her struggling, as she must have struggled before she became too weak. Perhaps it was her dying that one heard. And the footsteps were the release of her spirit, moving away.

Yet always towards the door. Now they would reach the door. Perhaps – who knew – he would see something go out.

They began. They were slower and heavier tonight. Every step was distinct, seemed to shake the room, measured itself with a thumping of his heart. He sat up sharply in bed, straining to the darker side of the room to see if he could see anything. A flickering flame from the fire, just like that other night, brought shadows to life in the silent room.

The footsteps reached five, reached six and appeared to hesitate. They were at the door. A seventh and then the fire did play tricks, for he saw the door quiver and begin to open. He screwed up his eyes, one hand pulling at the skinny flesh around his throat.

But there was no mistake. He *was* seeing something. The door was literally *opening* to allow something to go out. He could feel the difference in the air. The door was wide and something must be going out.

Then he twisted round in the bed, clutching at the rail behind him, trying to get up, to move away, to get out of bed and scream. Because round the door a hideous deformed face was appearing, with one eye, and the flesh drawn up and scarred, and a gash where the mouth should have been, and no recognisable nose.

It was clear then – quite clear – that moving the chair was not enabling Mrs Covent to go out. Captain Covent was coming in.

(v)

'It was always a possibility, of course,' said Dr Abrahams. 'The pulmonary oedema was an added complication. But I'm disappointed. He gave one the impression of great tenacity – great physical tenacity, I mean; such men can often endure more than ordinary people and yet recover and live to a great age.'

'Well, I can tell you it gave me the shock of my life,' said Agnes, drying her eyes. 'I came in at half past seven as usual and there he was half out of bed and clutching his throat. He seemed all right when I left him. We were a bit later than usual – about twelve it would be. I never heard a thing in the night. But he'd such an *expression* on his face.'

'He's been dead some hours. He probably died soon after you left him. I think the expression is due to the nature of the complaint: a sudden great pain, shortness of breath, no doubt he was trying to call you.'

'He had a bell there,' said Roy. 'It was on the table. Just there on the table. I'd have heard if he'd rung. I always sleep light.'

'Yes, well, there it is, there it is. His condition had been vaguely unsatisfactory all this last week, without there being anything one could necessarily pick on. I take it you're his nearest relatives?'

'His only relatives,' said Agnes. 'But he was well known in his circle. I think there will be a fair number of people at the funeral.'

(vi)
There were a fair number of people at the funeral. Representatives of societies with long names and short membership lists, club friends who had known Whiteleaf for a long time, one or two newspaper men, nominees from charities which had benefited in the past, some of Agnes's friends. It was a fine day, and the ceremony passed off well. After it, after a discreet interval, after a quiet period of mourning, Agnes and Roy burned the diary which had first put the idea into their heads. By discreetly opening it each afternoon while Uncle Julian was asleep, Agnes had been able to keep in touch with the progression of his thoughts.

At the same time they burned a rubber mask of humorously unpleasant appearance which Roy had bought in the toy department of a big store and painted and altered to look more hideous. There seemed no particular reason to burn the mop with which Agnes had bumped nightly on the ceiling beneath Uncle Julian's bedroom. Nor did they bother to burn the basket chair which Agnes had bought in a jumble sale and whose cane had the peculiarity of reacting with creaks and clicks about fifteen minutes after a person had been sitting in it, a peculiarity they had not noticed until Uncle Julian had drawn attention to it in his diary. It seemed a pity, Agnes said, to destroy a useful chair.

That spring they had their first real holiday for ten years. They went to the South of France for two weeks. Roy had considered giving up his railway job, but for the moment he was keeping it to see how much Uncle Julian's invested income brought in. On the way back from the South of France they spent two days in Paris, and Roy made inquiries about the film he was interested in. Later that year in Swindon he intended to give a private showing to his interested friends of *La Bête Humaine*.

IX

The Sad Ghost

R. Chetwynd-Hayes

Once they had moved into the house, Grandma had to admit it wasn't half bad, and the garden was an ideal place to have tea on a hot, summer afternoon. In fact, she made her son buy a nice green enamel table and four comfortable folding chairs, then ordered a multi-coloured garden umbrella from a mail-order firm that had had the foresight to insert an advertisement in *The Silver Thread Home Companion*.

John Smith waved his teaspoon in the direction of the house and said complacently: 'You've got to admit it looks picturesque.'

And indeed it did. With its red-tiled roof, mellow brickwork, five white-framed windows up and four down, a neat green door in the centre and rambling roses making a gallant effort to reach the freshly painted guttering, it looked as every country house should, but rarely does.

Sorel – who had yet to recover from a most unsatisfactory love affair – sighed and said: 'The house has a romantic atmosphere. It's sort of seeped in time.'

John made a disgusting derogatory sound and Ethel laughed.

'Don't get so emotional, dear. You won't sleep tonight.'

Sorel blushed and gave the impression she might burst into tears, if given the slightest encouragement. But Grandma nodded, then adjusted her glasses and examined the house with critical interest.

'The child's right. Old houses have their memories, just like people. Some sad, and a few that don't bear thinking about. And here in the country it's so quiet.'

John Smith – as behoved a practical, get-ahead business man – frowned, laughed (if a trifle uneasily) and said:

'It's not like you to be so fanciful, Mother.'

The old lady glared at him and crumbled a morsel of seed cake between the forefinger and thumb of her right hand.

'Just because I'm pushing seventy and likes me spot of bingo, don't mean I haven't an intelligent thought in my head. Which is more than can be said for some people.'

John Smith smiled indulgently and winked at Ethel, an action which did not pass unnoticed by his mother, who nodded slowly as though arriving at a reluctant conclusion. She turned her head and examined her son's pudgy face, which was framed by fashionable long hair, then that of her daughter-in-law who, at forty-six, was fighting with the armoury provided by art to retain the remnants of her youthful prettiness. They are so ordinary, she thought. But Sorel was another matter. Her beauty was quite breathtaking, even if she was still a child at eighteen. The sad grey eyes looked into her own and she sighed deeply.

'You poor pretty dear.' The unspoken words slid across her brain. 'Don't fret. This, too, will pass.'

That was the hard-won wisdom that old age carried on its bent shoulders. All life was transient. The peak of ecstasy, the agonizing hell of depression – all would pass and become elusive ghosts of memory that receded along the misty avenue of time. Today's purple tragedy became tomorrow's amusing anecdote.

Having reached this conclusion, Grandma fell asleep. She had not intended to do so, being of the opinion that only lazy people slept during the hours of daylight, but a combination of heat, sound (the rattle of teacups, the hum of an inquisitive bee) and the cumulative effect of three restless nights, was too much for her tired old brain and body.

However, she was dimly aware that Ethel and Sorel were clearing away the tea things and John had wandered off on some mission of his own; even heard her daughter-in-law say: 'Let her sleep. She's looked so tired lately.' Then she was suddenly wide awake, alone under the multi-coloured umbrella, muttering fearfully: 'No ... it mustn't happen ... ' and staring up at one particular window.

It was the first one on the left. Four well-cleaned panes of glass that now reflected the amber light of the setting sun. Grandma shook her head, ordered her dangerously thudding heart to behave itself and spoke words of self-reproach.

'Maggie, don't be such a silly old fool.'

But she could not dismiss the perfectly ridiculous notion that some time during that perilous period which separates sleep from wakefulness, a face had been looking down at her from that window. The face of someone long dead.

Sorel insisted that she be moved into the end bedroom, maintaining it received an early ration of sunlight in the morning and commanded a fine view of the distant hills. Ethel and John complained about the extra work such a move entailed, and Grandma said that when she was young, a girl remained in whatever room was offered her – and was properly grateful. But, of course, the child was allowed to have her own way; the collection of records, books, large posters (some of which the old lady thought rather disgusting), to say nothing of two wardrobes, one chest of drawers and one bed, were transferred to the new location.

Grandma inspected the end result.

'It's a bit smaller than the one down the landing,' she commented, 'and so far as I can see the view's no different.'

The girl stood by the fireplace, a wing of auburn hair half hiding her face. 'But I like it better than any other room in the entire house. And – I know this must sound silly – but it's sort of lonely. The very walls seem to be pleading for company.'

The old lady said: 'Ah!' twice and moved over to the window, where she stared down into the garden. She saw the striped umbrella and the empty chairs and shook her head.

'That's plain daft,' she murmured.

'I know.' Sorel's voice came from behind her. 'But that's the way I feel. But don't tell Mum or Dad. They wouldn't understand.'

'But I do?'

'Yes. Because they're middle-aged, but you're not really old. Not deep inside.'

And she kissed Grandma's cheek and in consequence stopped the old lady from asking questions that in all probability would not have received satisfactory answers.

Instead she said: 'Go along with you. The chances are you'll be calling me a silly old coot before the week's out,' then hurried from the room like a young girl who has just been paid her first compliment. Later – in the sleepless hours that precede dawn – she allowed thoughts to form tiny pyramids of conjecture; sent out mental feelers through the silent house and tasted the loneliness, the sadness – and the rising wave of hope. She created a warning from whispered words.

'Be careful. The purring kitten soon forgets.'

She sensed, rather than heard the low laugh.

John Smith was of the opinion that it was about time his daughter pulled herself together and stopped moping in her room and went out and about, maintaining that this was the correct conduct for persons of her age and sex. Of course Ethel, being a dutiful wife, fully endorsed this statement and expressed the belief that there were more well-endowed, better-looking and constant fish in the sea, than had as yet been taken out. Sorel listened with praiseworthy attention, waited until both parents had exhausted their immediate fund of wisdom, then made utterance.

'I've decided that men are not worth worrying about. They're selfish, sloppy and have only one thought in their tiny minds.'

Ethel cast a quick glance at her husband and appeared to be pondering on this point of view.

'I won't say, dear, there isn't something in what you say, but that's no reason why you shouldn't get out and about. Go to a nice social. Join the local youth club. I'm sure there must be one somewhere.'

'Oh, leave me alone.'

The girl ran from the room as Ethel expelled a deep, exasperated sigh, and John frowned and would doubtlessly have expressed a profound opinion had not Grandma interrupted from her chair by the window.

'The girl's reached an awkward age. At eighteen you don't know which way the wind's blowing. Leave her to me.'

'Be careful what you say,' Ethel warned. 'You can be so tactless sometimes.'

The old woman ignored the remark and watched the living-room door, which at that particular moment was slowly opening of its own accord. No one else appeared to notice this slightly disturbing phenomenon, and there was really no valid reason why she should draw their attention to it. The word 'draught' crept across her mind, although there was not so much as a breeze to disturb the tall grass at the bottom of the garden. But Grandma narrowed her eyes and flirted with the possibility that something which had been only a memory shadow was being reinforced by raw, adolescent energy. Such an idea was complete nonsense, of course, but it seemed to slip out from a dark cavern in her brain and would not be dismissed. And she discovered that, once embarked on this road of conjecture, there was no turning back. If – her limited vocabulary was not adequate to allow her to translate such a subject into words – two beings shared a common sorrow, then surely they would be drawn together. Each one attempting to comfort the other – only the girl would soon recover.

Grandma creased her face into a deep frown and got up.

'About time I peeled them potatoes,' she announced and trotted into the kitchen, much to the astonishment of Ethel, who had never been given this kind of assistance before. A few minutes later the living-room door slammed, and John was heard to remark that he hoped the house wasn't subsiding.

Three days later, the Smiths, in an effort to further the process of forcing their daughter to get out and about, threw a small party. True, their circle of acquaintances was still somewhat limited, but the vicar, being himself a newcomer to the district, was more than pleased to put in an appearance and pretended to be vastly amused when the local doctor said he had yet to blunt his scalpel on a human soul. Youth was represented by the nephew of Mrs Carrington-Smythe – secretary of the Self Employed People's Party – a receding chinned, not-much-to-say-for-himself young man who stared at Sorel with inarticulate admiration and blushed unbecomingly when she smiled at him.

Having gathered together a number of people who normally would have passed one another in the street without exchanging so much as a nod, John found himself with a well-nigh insurmountable problem as to what to do with them. He assumed a hearty, let's-have-fun expression and took up a position by the sideboard, which bore more than a passing resemblance to a miniature off-licence.

'What will it be?' he enquired. 'Mrs Carrington-Smythe – can I tempt you?'

'I never indulge,' that lady replied. 'If you have a grapejuice I might consider it.' She addressed the entire assembly. 'I always maintain that strong drink is the crutch required by the morally crippled. Do you not agree with me, Vicar?'

The Reverend Waters, who had been casting appreciative glances in the direction of the whisky decanter, could only agree, and even went so far as to suggest that the road to hell was quite possibly flanked by empty bottles. However, Miss Jenkins – a strong-willed lady who ran the village Post Office – said her morals were in fine shape and she'd like a port and lemon. Thereupon Sorel giggled and nudged Arnold Carrington-Smythe, a course of action which made that young man blush to an even deeper shade of red and stare earnestly at the carpet.

From that time onward, conversation was hard to come by. The doctor did try to drum up some enthusiasm about the exceptionally fine weather, but Miss Jenkins stated emphatically it wouldn't last. Then John started to describe the house improvements he intended to carry out in the near future, but, as he was not gifted with a fertile imagination, this subject failed to excite anyone's interest. Finally it was Mrs Carrington-Smythe who relit the conversational fire.

'I suppose you know this house has a bad reputation?'

There was an immediate favourable reaction. The vicar

assumed an air of professional interest, being under the impression the lady was referring to some past history of unsavoury conduct; the doctor smiled indulgently, and Miss Jenkins nodded grimly, as though she knew much but was prepared to allow someone else to unveil the face of truth. Grandma sighed and took a tiny sip from her gin and lime.

'Bad reputation!' Ethel gasped. 'Whatever do you mean?'

Mrs Carrington-Smythe flicked an imaginary speck from her blue serge skirt and gave the impression she was about to perform a painful duty with great reluctance.

'I only know what I've been told, and doubtlessly the story has gained much in the telling. But there is rarely smoke without fire, no matter how small the flames, and it might be as well if you were told by someone who prides herself on having a fund of common sense. One fact is beyond dispute. A young man committed suicide in this house.'

The vicar said: 'Good gracious!' this being the strongest expletive he could use in mixed company; the doctor exclaimed: 'Indeed!' and Miss Jenkins said nothing at all, only nodded again, then drained her glass of port and lemon. Arnold allowed his mouth to drop open, while Sorel looked rather bored. Grandma asked: 'Why?'

Mrs Carrington-Smythe frowned. 'Why what?'

'Why did he do himself in?'

'He was crossed in love.' Miss Jenkins supplied the answer. 'The squire's daughter jilted him, and he drank prussic acid.'

The secretary of the Self Employed People's Party raised her voice. She did not take kindly to anyone who tried to steal her thunder.

'You have been misinformed. The girl was his second cousin and he hanged himself.'

'Squire's daughter,' Miss Jenkins insisted. 'Prussic acid.'

'Speaking for myself,' the doctor commented, 'I'd favour the rope. Prussic acid would be very nasty. No woman would be worth that.'

Mrs Carrington-Smythe turned her slightly bovine eyes in his direction. Her voice sounded not unlike a knife being drawn across ice.

'You must remember, Doctor, that this event took place at the turn of the century, when young people were not afflicted by the lack of moral fibre that appears to be the curse of the present up-and-coming generation. In those days, when a young man fell in love with a gal, he loved her, and no bones about it. Dare I say that men were men and not prone to flinch from a bottle of prussic acid?'

'Or a length of clothes line,' Miss Jenkins added.

Neither of the ladies appeared to have realized that they had – so to speak – exchanged ends, and they continued to glare one at the other, until Ethel said:

'Well, thank goodness it all happened a long time ago. Let's hope the young man found peace at last – no matter how he ended his life.'

There was a short, pregnant silence before Mrs Carrington-Smythe dropped her well-primed bombshell.

'Yes – well, that's the crux of the matter. According to local tradition he did not find peace. He's still ...'

'Very restless,' Miss Jenkins interrupted. 'There are those who say he's been seen looking out through one of the windows ...'

'Standing on the front doorstep,' Mrs Carrington-Smythe corrected. 'Looking out over the fields ...'

'Over the garden.' Miss Jenkins was doing her best to deal kindly with the misinformed. 'Waiting for his unfaithful loved one to return.'

The doctor expressed an unfortunate opinion.

'I've never heard so much piffle in all me born days. If you ask me, the entire story was invented by a crowd of old women with nothing better to do. Good God!'

There is nothing like an attack from a third party to turn two former enemies into a close alliance. Miss Jenkins and Mrs Carrington-Smythe both rose and moved slowly, but with great dignity, towards the door. Ethel, mindful that her reputation as a hostess demanded she make some conciliatory overtures, all but ran after the departing guests and tried to pour oil on exceedingly troubled waters.

'Please, I'm sure the doctor did not mean to offend you. He spoke without thinking.'

As though to deny any lapse of thought on his part, the doctor's voice bellowed from the drawing-room.

'Both mad, you know. A pair of frustrated old hens.'

Miss Jenkins gasped, and Mrs Carrington-Smythe called out to Arnold, who appeared to be riveted to his seat beside Sorel.

'Arnold, come here this instant. We are leaving.'

The donning of coats, the gathering of handbags and umbrellas, even the opening of the front door – all such mundane actions were performed without words, until Miss Jenkins was about to step down into the small drive. Then she turned round and glared at Ethel and John.

'I hope your hair turns white,' she hissed.

The ill-fated party broke up soon afterwards.

In the days which followed, Grandma kept her thoughts to herself, but watched Sorel with anxious eyes. The girl appeared to be more cheerful than before the night of the party and even discussed the possibility of getting a job with the local pharmacist, but the old woman detected an almost indefinable air of detachment, periods of dreamy unawareness, that were followed by a kind of unnatural gaiety.

'It's nice to see her more like her old self,' Ethel remarked, and John lit his pipe and sent out fat smoke rings and watched them rise to the ceiling.

'She'll soon be out and about.'

Then one evening Grandma received confirmation of her suspicion, and anxiety was transformed into fear-tinted pity.

She came out of her bedroom, walked the entire length of the landing, and was about to descend the stairs when she became aware of a figure standing by Sorel's door. For the space of five seconds she did not fully understand who or what it could be, was, in fact, on the verge of ignoring it – dismissing the imperfect memory of a tall young man from her mind.

Then knowledge flared up into a bright flame, and she *knew*.

Slowly, with great reluctance, Grandma turned her head and accepted the evidence presented by her old eyes. The face could have been classified as handsome were it not for the weak chin: the eyes were well shaped, dark, melancholy, the body slender to the point of leanness. He was dressed in a grey cutaway coat, white shirt and what in Grandma's young days had been called drainpipe trousers. The general impression was one of instability; an affection-starved mind married to a frail body.

Then he smiled. A slow baring of white teeth, a flash of joy in the dark eyes, the transformation of despair into the hope of ultimate fulfilment. Grandma shook her head and said: 'No – it won't work,' and found she was alone, facing an unresponsive expanse of white-painted door. Presently she continued her interrupted journey down the stairs.

During dinner, Ethel and John tossed remarks at each other across the roast lamb, and Sorel toyed with her food and seemed totally unaware of Grandma's furtive glances. Then the plates and dishes were cleared away and it was time to watch television, a pastime that the old lady usually enjoyed, only now she had a problem to solve that any self-respecting script editor would have rejected as 'lacks credibility.'

At first she was tempted to share the burden of her knowledge, but after some little consideration decided that neither son nor daughter-in-law were equipped to deal with the unusual. John would more than likely treat the revelation as an outrageous joke, and Ethel would most certainly have a fit of hysterics. As for Sorel – how much did she know at the present time? Youth hugged its secrets and was able to accept the bizarre with surprising equanimity. No, she must wait, watch, be prepared to act when the time was right.

Sleep is a little death, and it is a matter for enthralling conjecture where that atom of consciousness we call the soul goes during the period when the body rests. It is reasonable to suppose that the young visit some pleasure city that is not far removed from the material plane, whereas the old must surely stray across the frontier that separates the quick from the dead. Conversely, they may never wander more than a few yards from their beds, always prepared to re-enter the house of flesh when the heart misses a beat or danger approaches.

Grandma was suddenly wide awake.

She lay listening, trying to remember what had disturbed her, straining her ears, peering across the room, which was saved from total darkness by moonlight filtered through the drawn curtains. After a while she switched on the bedside lamp, fumbled for her spectacles, then gave a loud sigh of relief when the familiar furniture came into clear focus. Light is a great comforter.

The low, rippling laugh was almost imperceptible, and the old woman might not have heard it had she not attuned her ears to detect the slightest sound. Her body was reluctant to leave the warm bed, and the dressing-gown slipped from her rheumatic-stiff fingers, so that she had to bend down and pick it up, before forcing her arms into the quilted sleeves. Then there was difficulty in finding one slipper, but finally it was located, lurking under the dressing-table stool – and she was ready to perform the most courageous act of her life.

A thin ribbon of light marked the bottom of Sorel's bedroom door, and scarcely had Grandma placed her ear against one panel when the low laugh again disturbed the night silence. Then she heard Sorel say: 'This is ridiculous. Really it is.'

The old woman gripped the brass handle, turned it and flung the door back. Sorel, attired in light blue pyjamas, was on the bed, which was situated to the right of the doorway, and, at the moment when Grandma entered, was lying on her left side and facing the fireplace wall. She turned a startled face and glared back over one shoulder.

'What do you want?'

There was no sign of an intruder, and the old woman did not really expect to see one. She supposed, without giving the matter much thought, that her entrance had disturbed the atmosphere, dispersed whatever energy was necessary to build him up, and brought about a temporary oblivion. Sorel slipped off the bed and, after casting one quick glance in the direction of the fireplace, began to protest with all the ardour of a child who has been indulging in some forbidden pastime.

'You've no right to burst in like this. I've got some right to privacy, haven't I?'

'You mustn't encourage him,' Grandma said quietly. 'You're playing with fire.'

'I don't know what you mean. You're just a silly old woman.'

Grandma closed the door behind her, then seated herself on the bed. She was horrified to find her knees were knocking together.

'Don't play the innocent with me. I know exactly what's going on, and it's got to stop.'

Sorel's eyes widened in astonishment as she sank into a chair.

'You ... you know!'

'You little fool – I've seen him.'

Two tears seeped out from Sorel's eyes and rolled slowly down her smooth cheeks. Grandma thought she wept beautifully.

'Perhaps,' she said softly, 'you'd better tell me how it all began.'

The young voice clothed the bizarre with matter-of-fact words.

'I liked this room because it suited my mood. You know – I was so unhappy about – you know who. I suppose I knew someone – or something – was here, but never actually thought much about it. Not, that is to say, until those two old biddies told that story about the ghost. Then – I sort of called him up. Is that the right expression?'

'It will do,' Grandma replied grimly. 'But how did you set about it?'

Sorel smoothed her hair with one white hand.

'Well, I thought about him for a bit. Then tried to imagine what he looked like ... then sort of pictured him standing by the window ... and what do you know? He was.'

Grandma shuddered and decided she would never

understand the young generation.

'Good grief, girl! Didn't you scream? Faint, or something?'

Sorel wiped her eyes and giggled.

' 'Course not. Honestly, Grandma, you are square. I mean, it was so thrilling and quite took me out of myself. A real ghost and rather dishy, even if he did look so sad. Gosh, I know girls who'd give their eye-teeth for an experience like that.'

'Which only goes to show they haven't been brought up properly. What happened next?'

'I tried to talk to him, because I read somewhere you're supposed to talk to ghosts. But at first he was so shy.'

Grandma frowned. 'At first! I take it he became more forthcoming later?'

Sorel tilted her head to one side and appeared to give the question some thought. Then she said:

'I suppose you could say so. He never speaks – perhaps he can't. But he stands and looks at me and appears to understand what I'm saying. He's got a lovely smile.'

'And what do you say?' the old lady demanded.

'Oh, this and that. How awful I think that girl was who jilted him, and how, if he feels lonely, I don't mind talking to him. You know.'

'But it's got to stop. Do you hear me, girl? You mustn't encourage him.'

Sorel pouted, and Grandma thought how beautiful, spoilt and wilful she looked.

'Why? I mean it's not as though he was a real person. Well – not a flesh-and-blood person. He can't do me any harm.'

Grandma got up. 'I'm not so sure that I'm all that concerned about you. It's the ghost I feel sorry for. Am I to understand he'll materialize – or whatever he does – the moment I turn my back?'

'No. You spoilt everything by bursting in like that. I bet it will be days before he comes back again. He's very sensitive, you know. That row at the party upset him dreadfully.'

Grandma cast an apprehensive glance around the room.

'Well, that's as maybe. But listen to someone who knows what she's talking about. Get rid of him. Tell him to shove off.

It will be kinder in the long run. What your mother would say if she knew you were playing footsy with a ghost doesn't bear thinking about.'

'You won't tell her?'

Grandma opened the door and peered out on to the landing. There was always the possibility that the phantom lover had been eavesdropping_

'Don't be daft. I wouldn't tell her the time of day. Now, remember what I said. Send him about his business.'

'Grandma – you're sweet.'

'I know. But don't tell anyone.'

The old are ordained to give advice, and the young have a duty to reject it.

Although Grandma heard no sounds from Sorel's room during the dark hours, she knew instinctively the girl was still entertaining her spectral swain. She sighed deeply and not for the first time tried to imagine how the affair would end. Fortunately, Sorel was displaying signs of returning normality; she applied for and obtained a post as typist in the nearby town and went to the cinema twice a week, so that her parents became quite optimistic.

'Next thing you know,' John observed, 'she'll be bringing a young spark home. One that will appreciate her.'

Grandma shuddered.

Of course he was absolutely right. One Sunday evening the rural peace was disturbed by the roar of a particularly ferocious-looking motor-cycle, and Sorel was seen to dismount from the pillion seat and lead a tall young man with a big nose towards the front door. Ethel withdrew her face from the drawn back curtain and exclaimed:

'John, put your jacket on. Sorel has brought a young man home.'

John said it was about time, and Grandma pretended she did not hear a door slam upstairs.

Later she learnt that the young man was burdened with the name of Jason Butterworth, that he was a with-it-and-get-out-and-find-it tearaway, who beat a drum in the local pop group.

It was a case of hate at first sight. He had a mass of frizzed blond hair and an unkempt beard, and wore an exotic line in shirts and a big brass medallion. He also – when introductions were made – addressed Grandma as 'Gran'.

She knew with a dreadful certainty that they would never get on together. But Ethel, who believed in milking all prospective son-in-law material of any relevant information in the shortest possible time, smirked, poured tea into the best green cups and sent out the first, tentative feeler.

'I expect a lovely motor-cycle like that costs a lot of money. I mean to say, you'd have to earn quite a bit to be able to afford it.'

Jason was not weighted down by modesty and supplied the correct answer in no time at all.

'S'right. If I wasn't pulling in a load of bread, I'd never be able to cock a leg over that baby.'

'Goodness gracious! John, ask Jason if he would like a slice of cream sponge.'

John was not all that taken by the newcomer. Such words as: 'Haircut', 'Shave', 'Good wash' and 'Spot of square-bashing' tripped across his mind, but in these hard days, when it has become almost impossible to meet a young man who is prepared to feed and support another man's daughter, no likely candidate can be dismissed out of hand. So he nudged the cake-stand in the direction of his guest and advanced the interrogation one important step.

'What's your occupation, son? Apart from beating a drum?'

Jason emptied his teacup and held it out for a refill before answering.

'Elevation operative.'

'How interesting!' Ethel exclaimed. 'Does that mean you promote people to higher positions?'

Sorel giggled. 'Mum, honestly! Jason drives a crane.'

The door opened suddenly and crashed against the side wall.

Everyone registered shocked surprise, save Grandma, who nodded grimly and tried to command Sorel's attention. John got up, muttering something about shifting bedrock, and

Jason, entirely unaware of the dangerous ground on which he was planting his clumsy feet, said: 'Don't tell me this place is haunted?' then laughed in a most disgusting fashion.

John closed the door as the milk jug nose-dived into Jason's lap.

The ensuing silence was broken by Grandma's sardonic voice.

'The ghost don't seem to fancy you.'

Ethel snapped: 'Grandma, that was uncalled for,' and hastened to the kitchen in search of a damp cloth, while Sorel glared her annoyance and gave the impression she would have some sharp words to say to someone, when a suitable occasion arose. Jason's trousers were cleaned – after a fashion – but although he appeared to accept the profuse apologies and even agreed worse things happen at sea, it was easy to see he wasn't all that happy. There was a tendency to watch the refilled milk jug, eye the door with grave suspicion and grin inanely whenever anyone spoke to him.

'The bloody thing jumped,' he said presently.

John frowned and tried to catch his wife's eye. He did not approve of bad language.

'Jumped! What jumped?'

'The flaming milk jug.'

'Rubbish. How can a milk jug jump?'

Jason left shortly afterwards, not forgetting to take Sorel with him. Barely had the front door closed when Ethel raised her head and took up the position of someone who is listening to a far-off sound.

'What's wrong now?' John demanded.

'Nothing ... Only, for a moment I thought I heard someone crying.'

The hall clock had struck two when Grandma, quite unable to subdue her curiosity, crept out on to the landing and flattened her ear against Sorel's bedroom door. The one-sided conversation was most enthralling.

'I'm not going to stand for it.' Sorel's voice had acquired a built-in nagging quality and Grandma thought she would make someone an excellent wife. 'Always hanging about looking like a slab of cold mist. And I'll go out with whom I please, and if I choose to bring them home, I don't expect you to slam doors or throw milk jugs. Are you listening to me?'

There was the sound of a muffled sob, the merest suggestion of a strangled word, before Sorel continued her tirade.

'I can understand why that other girl gave you the elbow. Was fed up to the front teeth, I wouldn't wonder. And what did you do? Hanged yourself – or drank something horrid. Silly great twit. When I was given the push-off treatment some time ago, I didn't do myself in. I just moped a bit, chatted you up – then went out and found Jason ... Don't you grit your teeth at me.'

Grandma chuckled, did a little dance and muttered: 'That's telling him.'

'And now – out. Get out of this house. Go and find yourself a ghost lady or something. Go on.'

He – it – materialized through the door, and Grandma retreated along the landing and took up a position by her own bedroom door, where she watched the apparition with grave concern. The white face was not so much sad as sullen; it had much in common with that of a husband who considers he has been grievously wronged. He glided rather than walked down the stairs and disappeared into the darkness-shrouded hall. A little later a soft thud suggested that the front door – which was securely locked – had been opened and closed.

Grandma went into Sorel's room and found the girl seated on her bed.

'Well,' she said quietly, 'you took my advice at last. He's gone.'

Sorel's eyes were bright with unshed tears.

'Oh, Grandma, if only he had had a little more go. Been just a teeny bit like Jason.'

Grandma tried to imagine a ghost that beat a drum and decided that, if she had to choose, one that sobbed was much preferable.

'Let's hope we've seen the last of him. Now, I'm going back to bed.'

Jason became a fairly regular visitor, and Sorel went out with him most nights of the week and every Saturday. It was understood she was thinking of learning to play the clarinet and had already mastered the basic rules of beating a drum. Ethel decided she would wear blue at the wedding, John was wondering if the bridegroom would share the expense of the reception, and Grandma announced she wanted nothing to do with the entire proceeding.

The sad ghost had apparently taken his dismissal to heart and no longer haunted Sorel's bedroom, a state of affairs that should have been a matter for quiet satisfaction, but Grandma sometimes heard her crying during the small hours. When questioned, the girl said: 'Aren't men stupid? Oh, I don't know what I want,' a statement that received the old lady's complete endorsement.

One Saturday afternoon, Grandma was dozing peacefully under the striped umbrella. John and Ethel had gone to Midminster to do some shopping, Sorel was doubtlessly being transported across the countryside on the back of Jason's motor-cycle, and it was pleasant to know that for a few hours there would be no one to disturb the sultry tranquillity of a summer afternoon. A large bluebottle buzzed round the old lady's head and brought her to the surface of consciousness. She waved an impatient hand and became aware of other sounds: the quarrelsome chatter of sparrows, the restless breeze that sighed through the leaves of the old elm tree – and the muted snarl of an approaching motor-cycle. She muttered: 'Damnation!' and resolved that she would pretend to be asleep, even, possibly, assume a death-like stillness that would surely frighten her granddaughter, if not the beater-of-drums-cum-elevation operative.

The snarling engine drew nearer, rose to a high-pitched scream – then suddenly ceased. Grandma opened her eyes and tried to understand why Jason should cut off his engine a hundred yards or so from the house. There was such a thing as consideration for elderly ladies who were having a quiet Saturday-afternoon nap, but she doubted if Jason would walk a hundred yards on that account. Of course, the motor-cycle may not have been his, but that of a perfect stranger who had chosen to indulge in some hanky-panky in Farmer Gamlin's field.

Having arrived at this conclusion, Grandma was about to close her eyes when she saw Sorel looking down at her from the extreme left-hand bedroom window. Afterwards, she remembered the expression of surprise, the slight frown, but at the time she was aware only of an irrational feeling of intense anger. It was as though the mere presence of the girl standing at her own open bedroom window was the result of an irresponsible action, that she, Grandma, had helped bring about.

She called out: 'What are you doing there?' and Sorel smiled and appeared to be trying to answer, only Grandma could not hear a word. Then Jason came lurching round a bend in the drive, his gaily coloured shirt stained with blood, his face as white as a slab of snow in moonlight, his mouth gabbling words that created a kind of mad logic.

'The silly bleeder was standing in the road ... I tried to miss him ... and went through him ... through him ...'

He collapsed at Grandma's feet, but the old woman could only stare up at the now-empty window, her anger replaced by an unexplainable feeling of comfort.

At last the sad ghost had acquired a bit of go. There was no reason to suppose he would ever be sad or lonely again.

Presently a car came purring up the drive and braked to a halt. Ethel and John got out.

X

In Spite of Himself

Giles Gordon

A man looked out of a window. His eyes searched the landscape in front of him.

He was in a room, his own room, on the second floor of a solid, stone two-storied house overlooking the harbour, packed at this time of year with the yachts and motor-launches of holidaymakers as well as with the usual fishing boats. The harbour was about three-quarters of a mile away from the house, down a steep hill. Mount Jason dominated the village, towered above it – usually serenely, occasionally darkly. And the house in which the man was, sat unobtrusively between village and mountain.

Half an hour ago the boats in the harbour and the village and the houses dotted along the coast were almost entirely blotted from view by grey sheets of rain and mist which seemed to absorb and devour ships, houses, people – even the sea itself. Staring out of the window the man could see nothing but dense greyness. The fact that the greyness was liquid, that had he been out of doors he could have walked into it and through it, didn't make it seem any less opaque.

The man's house, the house in which he was, appeared to be isolated from everybody and everything, and from time. He would not have been surprised, though he would have been frightened, had the thick greyness advanced upon the house, upon the windows of his room, and coated their surface so that he could not see – however he forced his eyes – the long wild and swaying grass in the garden, ten feet below him. The glass would then have ceased to be glass, would have become an impenetrable fourth wall; or a sixth, if the floor and ceiling were taken into account.

The windows of the room were, of course, securely closed. He didn't want the atmosphere contaminated by whatever floating properties there were in the rain and the mist. If the window continued to act as a wall, as a shield against the elements, through which he could peep while enduring the airless atmosphere of the room and the house, that would be tolerable. But if, somehow, the greyness managed to obtrude through the glass, ooze through the stone pores of the house, seep into the room, force itself into his body by way of his mouth and throat, or more cunningly through his nostrils or ears, cause him to choke and even suffocate, why then he might wonder why his past, his very life, had been necessary, why it should end in such a way.

But the greyness lifted. One moment it was there, the next not. Could he have imagined it? Yes, he could, of course he could, but he had not. The intensity of the experience, of the fear, was too great. He surveyed the landscape in front of him. The boats were all where they had been in the harbour – or they had been placed back there. The headland could clearly be seen, and the three promontories to the east, and the houses and fields in the foreground. The men who were building, reconstructing rather, a cottage about one hundred yards to the west of the house where the man was, reappeared (from where though?) and continued building. They were placing crossbeams on the roof. Because the roof was not yet solid, was not yet covered with tiles, had the builders been sheltering inside the shell of the cottage when the rain and foul weather was at its height, they could have been afforded no protection against the elements. And yet, the man noticed, their heads and their clothes were completely dry.

He had been looking out of the window for nearly an hour, though he was totally unaware of the passage of time that had elapsed since he began to look. At his age, and in this place, and his circumstances being what they were, what was the purpose of time other than to be passed? Not that he was that old, but he had seen younger years. His memories were of the past rather than that his anticipations were of the future. The present? It might as well not exist. It was always a time to be regretted in the future.

At first, he had just glanced out of the window. He hadn't moved towards it purposefully. He had looked out for no particular reason. Nothing had attracted his attention – a noise, for instance – and drawn him to the window, compelled him to look out.

He was alone in the house, in his own room. After he had been looking out for a minute or two, he couldn't withdraw his gaze, he couldn't stop looking. It was as if he knew something would happen out there, and he must witness it, even if it were not to occur for hours. He saw the changes in the weather – he pursued shadows with his eyes as they passed across the land and sea from east to west. He was aware of every shift of emphasis, of wind ruffling trees and hedges, of pieces of paper scurrying about. He observed and noted the few people who passed along the road in front of the house – towards the village and the harbour, or towards the solemn, lowering mountain behind the house. Not entirely idly, he wondered if those walking towards and into Mount Jason that day would ever reappear.

He took a positive, if negative, decision. He would try not to think. He consciously tried to keep his mind clear of thoughts. But more strenuously he attempted to avoid thinking, the more he found that random and inconsequential thoughts forced their way into his mind. He raised a hand to his head, tapped the crown three times with two finger tips, but this made no difference. His skull was still there. He was conscious of the existence, the reality of his mind. And, like tiny minnows, thoughts would creep in.

He wanted for a while not to think, not to have to think, because in recent years for almost every moment of consciousness he had been employed in thinking – however banal all but a few of these thoughts had been. His thinking usually took the form of worrying or fussing, but that was a kind of thinking, he felt certain. Thinking even made it difficult for him to sleep at nights. He would close his eyes, try to expel consciousness from the situation, and silly, trivial thoughts would steal in. And he would lie awake, achieving nothing but lack of sleep. Eventually, he would fall asleep – he assumed this happened because when he woke up it would be morning. But he would usually be exhausted.

Slowly, against his will, his judgement, his thought processes, he realized that in looking out of the window he *was* looking for something. For someone, in fact. The realization reluctantly came to him that he wasn't merely being idle, casually looking through the glass. There was a reason. In trying to deny this he had been deceiving himself, but not very successfully. He wasn't using the window and the view beyond and what happened in that view only as a kind of screen upon which to project and indulge his fancies and fantasies. The window, or rather what there was to see through it, also concerned his fears and ambitions.

Ambitions? He started. His eyebrows shot up, his head jerked back slightly. If he was thinking in these terms – if he was thinking at all – he was still in the present, once again hoping for a future. Could it be that there was no end? That without the self-destruction of the body – and this was something that he never had even in his darkest moments (and there had been plenty of those), never would, whatever the circumstances, countenance – hope, expectancy, ambition remained part of the self, an inevitable constituent of life? He did not want to hope, he no longer wished even for her presence. It was too painful to be hurt. In his youth he had thought – thought? no, assumed – that the older you grew the less vulnerable you became; the more the flesh decayed, the more the spirit could stand.

He passed the back of his right hand in front of his eyes, and sniffed. This was too stupid. He wouldn't become victim to human foibles. He would, again, be resolute. His eyes searched the landscape in front of him, close to the house, down to the sea, to east and to west as far as the windows allowed, the ground in between. In spite of himself. He did not wish to look. He was, somehow, forced, in spite of himself.

A sound stole into his consciousness. A little cry entered his awareness. At once he was drawn back in his mind to the house, to where he stood, to his present condition. He did not exist in a vacuum, on his own. He had forgotten: he was not alone. But, he asked himself, had he known? And if he had not, how could he have forgotten? There was another cry, or was it the first one, the previous one echoing, repeating in his mind? Had the first been an echo or a memory of a cry years ago, in time or out of time?

The baby slept in her cot below, in the bedroom on the ground floor. She was dreaming, if old enough to have the stuff of dreams, or whimpering in her sleep.

His thoughts, his fears, were concentrated on the cry, the sound, the baby. Still peering out of the window, his eyes wildly ploughed the landscape for a glimpse of her who would relate to his present predicament, comprehend and make sense of it. He couldn't or wouldn't articulate to himself, describe in his own mind, she for whom he was searching. He knew though that as soon as he saw her he would recognize her. Confrontation would be all that was necessary.

It was at this moment, not for the first time, that he couldn't remember his own name. His first name, yes. That he knew, instinctively, so long as he didn't have to utter it aloud. He wasn't sure that in those circumstances he'd be able to summon it into a word. But the occasion did not arise. Yet he had quite forgotten his surname, and as much thought and concentration as he was able to apply would not bring it back to him, would not reveal it. He was irritated. This was absurd. Everyone knew their names, even if they didn't know how to read and write. He knew that in time he would remember. He did not think that his name had gone for ever – had it done so, certainly he would have no identity – but the thought didn't console him in the least.

Once again he looked out of the window, or more precisely focused on what was there. He hadn't looked away at all, not even for a second, though while trying to dredge the memory of his name from whatever resources he had he might as well have done so. He had seen nothing. The landscape, village, harbour were all a blank. Now he saw what was in front of him as if it were a medieval illuminated manuscript, a painting from a book of hours. Everything was clear, sharp, intense, utterly in focus. He felt he understood it all, the secrets of the land were revealed in detail.

He observed, comprehending everything, but feeling apart, dispassionate. He watched the cows chewing, the pigs, horses, sheep. He noted which boats were leaving the harbour, which returning, who was chatting to whom outside Chambers' public house. He tried to stop thinking about his name. If he thought about something quite different, his name would most likely return to him. The baby had not called out again, or made a sound. At least he thought not, not that he had heard. He concentrated upon the silence in the house, listened for her breathing, but the wind was all he could hear. Besides, the exercise was absurd. The door of his room was closed, though not locked. It was surprising that he had heard the child's cry.

He frowned to himself, pouted his lips. Could he have heard the baby's cry through the closed door? The question did not arise, he realized: he *had* heard the cry, and that was that. He watched Mrs Hamilton and Albert (how old was he? Four?) Walk up from the village. Quite a conversation they were having. He was sufficiently interested, but for no particular reason, to wonder what about.

He knew that he should open the door of his room, go down and look at the baby, to see that she was well, but as she was not crying, she must be asleep, or lying there happily, or beyond help. What if the cry had been her last human gasp? The thought was ridiculous. Babies have to be tough to survive. At least there was no indication that she was hungry. He tried to concentrate his thoughts upon the baby downstairs, though, in spite of himself, he couldn't bring himself to go down and look at her. Nor, in his own mind, could he decide whether he was more afraid of finding her there, or that she had gone.

He closed his eyes, suddenly. He forced them to remain tight shut, locked together. Now he was no longer looking out of the window, at least not seeing. He had tricked himself, and perhaps the landscape outside. He had broken the spell, though as he thought this he realized how foolish it was even to think in such terms. Slowly, still with his eyes closed, he turned round to face the room. His back was to the window now. He opened his eyes, carefully, as if expecting the room to be populated with wild animals prepared to savage him, or people who bore him only ill will.

There was no one there. He expelled his pent-up breath, and allowed his taut frame, his hunched shoulders, to relax a bit. He was determined to retrieve his name. Without it he was a cipher, or less. Without a label, how could he have an identity? His eyes passed over the bookshelves against the wall opposite him, parallel to the windows. He would look at the fly leaf of a book. He must have written his name on a dozen or more volumes in the room, and it would appear on letters in the file to the right. There was the edition of Burns he had been awarded as a music prize at school all those years ago; and his mother's prayer book, passed on to him in her will. But knowing now that with ease he could reclaim his name, the few letters of the alphabet which gave him an identity, he ceased to be interested in this line of pursuit.

His eyes fell on a photograph album. *The* photograph album. He smiled to himself for a moment, and moistened his lips with his tongue. If he looked at the pictures of his wedding and saw himself there with her he would immediately know who he was, in spite of the lack of wrinkles on the young face in the photographs. Almost eagerly, almost displaying excitement and enthusiasm, he walked the few paces from the window to the bookcase. He pulled the album out from the row of books, and returned to the window. This time not to stand and look out, but to sit on a wicker armchair to the left of where previously he had been. He sat down, with the book in his lap.

The traces of the smile that had touched his lips and loosened the skin covering his cheekbones drained suddenly from his face. He discovered – remembered? — that he had forgotten not only his surname but his first name as well. Both names had gone, not to mention his two middle names which had also been the first two names of his father – that much he did remember. But what his father's name was he couldn't for the life, or death, of him remember.

He sunk deeper into the chair, seeming to forget the photograph album lying between his hands, certainly having forgotten that his name, and therefore also that of his father, was inscribed in probably dozens of books in the room in which he sat. The room seemed to be growing dark again, very quickly. It was as if a minute or two ago an electric light had been switched on, and when he wasn't looking had been clicked off. He looked up, out of the window. From his position in the chair, he couldn't see the land or sea, only the sky, but it was plain that the bad weather was returning, that the greyness was almost there. Rain at that moment would be pouring into the ground not further than two or three miles away. The realization filled him with a colossal, almost total, sense of dread and heaviness. He wasn't yet aware of it, but his body, face included, was bathed in sticky sweat.

He forced himself to look down at the photograph album, to open it. With a vacant, empty expression in his eyes, he turned over the first pages of babies, of young children with, as he saw it, preposterously young parents. Maybe it was one baby, the same baby at different stages of development. He began to turn the pages more and more quickly, with increasing impatience. He knew the wedding pictures were in the album but he couldn't remember where they came. It was years since he had looked at the book. No one else, least of all she, can have looked at it for a very long time either as the album was always on the shelves in his room and no one else entered the room. Who else would have kept it so spotless?

He turned the heavy grey pages over, and over. Some of the faces he half recognized, at least sensed that he had once known their owners. Eventually, he reached the pictures of a wedding, and his spirits rose slightly, his heart fluttered. He was expectant, as if he knew he would discover something in addition to his name. There was a large group, thirty or forty people, outside the door of a church. How archaic their clothes looked, even the bride's dress, and those of the bridesmaids. He had thought that such garments remained, if not exactly the height of fashion, the same for ever.

He smiled, with satisfaction, a sense of relief. There he was, himself, in the front row, near the centre, standing next to the bride. He stared at the picture, his eyes opening wide, the lids forcing themselves apart. The colour again fled from his face, the perspiration increased. His fingers trembled as he held the page. That wasn't her, standing next to him. That was Christine, his brother John's wife. And her arm was wound round John, not around him. He looked at himself again, his picture. He was standing, on his own, with a bridesmaid by his other side. He could tell this by her absurd costume.

Quickly he turned the page, hiding the photograph, trying to block it from his mind, trying not to make it part of his memory. He kept turning, almost without seeing what was on each page. There were other photographs of John's wedding, at which he had been best man. They seemed interminable, these pictures, all those shining, glossy faces. And his too, his own. Every time he caught a glimpse of his young, onetime features he was grinning inanely like the rest of them. It wasn't John's wedding he was looking for. Of course not. Even John would have known that, he thought bitterly. But he also knew that it was the only wedding portrayed in the photograph book, the only one of which there were pictures in the house. He reached the last page, and was confronted with the back cover. He closed the album slowly, with care, as if handling a baby. He stood up, and placed the book on the seat of the chair he had just vacated.

He looked out of the window, his heart almost missing a beat as he did so. He hadn't spent more than five minutes looking at the book, yet the weather that had been two or three miles away was upon him. Two hundred yards out there the rain and smoke or mist or fog or whatever it was rolling towards the house again. It was coming nearer and nearer. It didn't appear to be moving, to be projected forward by any external force, or by itself, but it was advancing fast, relentlessly. Obviously neither human nor an animal, it was as if it possessed life, as if it was in the very process of creating life, of becoming alive; and at the same time as if it was extinguishing life elsewhere, as if it could only progress beyond its own inchoate form by exterminating some more advanced being whose path it would cross. There was an inevitability about it. His eyes opened wider and wider. His mouth opened, and closed. Sweat poured off his forehead into his eyes but still he could not blot it from his vision. It advanced, kept advancing. He could now see only about one hundred feet, then fifty, then thirty, twenty, ten feet.

The glass was there to protect him, but it would be of little protection, he realized, if it – whatever it was – was determined to enter the house, his room, determined to destroy him. He forced his eyes to try to see beyond it, to see if she was coming, but he could see not a thing, not a shadow nor a silhouette, no land, no sea, certainly not a human being, not she who alone could save him. It was dark outside, dark way beyond dusk and becoming browner, blacker with every fraction of a second that passed.

His eyes still riveted to the glass, to what was still beyond, he moved his body a step towards the chair. He bent down sufficiently to pick up the photograph album. He pulled it towards him, and with both hands clutched it, as if it was his most prized possession, as if he would take it with him to the grave. At once he was filled with horror at the realization of what – he now knew – was about to happen. Somehow the book slid out of his soaking hands. The noise of the album hitting the floor caused him to jump, and a tremor passed through his whole body as if a gun had been fired close to his eardrum. It didn't even occur to him that the noise was the book striking the floor.

The room grew darker, darker. Outside, the noise of the thunder was so regular that it seemed to be one extended low roar. He staggered back from the window, then slowly, reluctantly lifted his right arm and hand towards the glass, as if to stop it advancing – whatever, whoever it was – as if to blot it out, expunge it, kill it.

His finger tips touched the glass, and the contact of a tiny, sensitive area of his body with the window – and by inference and in fact with what was beyond – was, simply, too much for him. He might have passed out, fainted, even suffered a heart attack on the spot. Instead, he leapt back into the room, at the same time uttering a horrifying cry, a sound of utter fear.

He cringed and winced backwards into the room, like an animal propelled back after hitting a live electric fence, until his body was upright and flat against the wall opposite the window – or what had until a moment before been the window.

The room was now not only black, black beyond the colour black, but he could see none of the walls, nor the glass, nor ceiling, nor floor. He only half assumed he was still in the room, on *terra firma*, because he could feel, or thought he could, the texture of the wall behind him with the drenched and dripping palms of his hands.

He closed his eyes, then opened them, then couldn't tell whether his eyes were open or shut. Then he ceased to feel the wall there, and his hands were flailing in space. His feet were no longer on the ground. But he wasn't flying, or falling through space.

He knew that whatever it was had entered the room, the house, and had utterly enveloped it. His room, the house, himself were being devoured, destroyed. He could only wait, wait for what was to come. Then something hit his face, and he was too afraid to wipe away the viscous liquid in which he seemed to be·drowning.

Suddenly, there was silence. He could only hear his breath, feel his ribs and his sore, exhausted body. Downstairs, if it still was downstairs, or ever had been, a baby began to cry.

XI

The Walking Shadow

Jean Stubbs

Tom Beaumont died on his twelfth oyster, which was a bad one and cost the tavern a number of its customers in the next few months. The oyster was not entirely to blame. Add eleven others, and a pint and a half of white wine, to a corpulent gentleman in his late fifties who has lived too well. Join this to the excitement of a successful first night in a play by Mr Wycherley. Throw in a tableful of good company, toasting stout Tom Beaumont as the greatest actor-manager in the city. And one faulty Whitstable becomes the last step between this world and the next.

In the eighteenth century the church considered theatres to be licensed dens of iniquity, and their players offshoots of the devil, so there seemed to be no point in summoning the clergy while Tom gasped on the dirty floor of the tavern. But Sarah Beaumont – Tom's wife, and a fine actress if somewhat overblown – found a drunken doctor, who finished off Tom's wine, bled him freely and applied leeches in a lavish and haphazard fashion to his person. In spite of this treatment and several spoonfuls of *Daffy's Elixir* Tom did not rally, but died with an actor-manager's philosophy on his lips.

'The theatre is all!' he whispered, and expired on the final syllable in great style: one splendid hand outflung, his Roman profile nobly turned to its best side.

He was buried in unconsecrated ground, which made Sarah cry though Tom would not have cared tuppence about it. Whether the church's censure made any difference to his state, or whether Tom would have refused to lie down in the holiest ground available, is not known. But he walked. It took him about a year to achieve his first appearance and he made it a notable one. White's Theatre was crammed from roof to floor, and deep in conversation, when Tom Beaumont materialised before the curtain, bowing graciously. For a moment they took him to be the new manager, Ned Bellamy, and clapped encouragement. Then a gentleman of the court leaned forward in his box and lifted his eye-glass. He took in the famous stance, one corpulent leg a little in advance of the other, one hand on the extravagantly ruffled cravat, the other behind the brocade coat. He recognised the florid countenance, the foppish wig, the vain little black eyes.

'Damme!' said the gentleman, aghast. 'If it isn't Beaumont!'

The spirit seemed to possess his hearing, since he turned and bowed to the box in a gratified manner. The gentleman bowed back automatically, and Beaumont vanished, leaving chaos behind him. Unlike most shades he had been seen on a grand scale: not by one hysterical female on a dark night, not by a frightened child in the grip of imagination, not by the simple, the gullible or the easily persuaded. Beaumont's ghost was viewed by an entire theatre audience, and the first act of *The Careless Husband* went for nothing.

Perhaps the restless dead, like the restless living, have a spiritual pilgrimage to make and must learn to conquer their personal vices before they can experience peace. Certainly Tom Beaumont resented his death, and resolved to harass the living as much as possible. He never forgave Sarah for marrying again, though he must have known that her generosity of body and heart made single life impossible. A buxom thirty-five, she gave her hand and a large share of White's Theatre to the new actor-manager, Ned Bellamy, less than a year after Tom's decease. By one of those inexplicable laws pertaining to ghosts, Tom was only allowed to haunt the theatre – perhaps because his own heart had been wholly there. So the new Mrs Bellamy was able to enjoy her second husband's bed and company undisturbed at home. At the theatre she entered upon a series of incidents which were finally to drive her into retirement.

The first, beautifully timed, occurred one month after her remarriage when she was gracing White's stage as Hamlet's mother. The closet scene had always been one of her best, but that evening she unwittingly surpassed herself. As Mr Dishart, in the role of the Prince, reproached her in ringing tones, Sarah saw Tom Beaumont materialise beside him. It was a purely personal visitation, since Mr Dishart gestured through Tom without noticing his presence, and the audience were disturbed by nothing stranger than Sarah's hysteria. She, horrified, put both hands over her mouth and began to walk backwards, whispering 'No, no, no,' into her tragedienne's black gloves. Mr Dishart, inwardly cursing all actresses of consequence, attempted to follow her up. But Tom came with him, and Sarah retreated so piteously – and so very near to the wings – that Mr Dishart stopped.

The admiration of the audience was tempered with some concern, as Hamlet – kept at a difficult distance – first repeated his cues, then hissed Sarah's lines, and finally carried on without her. And as he reviled the Queen for stewing in corruption, and making love over the nasty sty, Tom nodded belligerently. Reassured by the magnificent voice of Mr Dishart, and Sarah's brilliant exhibition of terror and remorse, the spectators decided that Mr Bellamy had improved on Mr Shakespeare by cutting the Queen's speeches. Anxious to be in the vanguard of this latest innovation, they applauded so long and loudly that Sarah had to appear before them again and again: her eyes inflamed by smelling salts. In spite of idolatrous reviews she never dared play Queen Gertrude afterwards.

One by one, Tom plucked the laurel leaves from her good-natured brow. His campaign and her increasing flesh shortened her career. She made her last appearance on the English stage as Lady Macbeth.

Tom chose to reveal himself in the sleepwalking scene, and his timing was – as always – superb. As Sarah cried, 'All the perfumes of Arabia will not sweeten this little hand!' he rose grinning at her side, saying, 'Nor all the stays in the world lessen this vast girth! Madam, you have growed uncommonly fat!'

Forty years later, when other Lady Macbeths chilled the blood of their admirers, old men would say, 'Why sir, you should have seen *Mrs Bellamy* in the sleepwalking scene. She groaned as if her heart was broke, I do assure you!'

Sarah lived until the age of seventy-five, secure and comfortable unless she set foot in White's Theatre. And Tom kept his resentment warm to the last, but he was cheated of her company. She died respectably, with a clear conscience and the blessing of the church, and never joined him.

With his wife off the boards, however, Tom turned his attention to Ned Bellamy, who was making a name for himself as a fine producer of Shakespearian tragedies. Now Shakespeare had a fondness for spectres, and gave them his maximum attention. Who could overlook Banquo's ghost at the feast, prevent a shiver as Caesar's helmeted shade strode the bloody battlefield at Philippi, or ignore Hamlet's father's spirit in the opening scene of that play? Tom cast himself in these roles with a zest that approached ruthlessness. He even took the trouble to delay or temporarily disable the actor cast for the part, lest the necessary impact be lost.

Ned Bellamy was playing Brutus when Tom made his debut towards the end of *Julius Caesar*. Stricken dumb with recognition, the audience were held captive while Ned Bellamy whispered, 'Speak to me what thou art.' Tom's powers were limited. He would have loved to boom out, 'Thy evil spirit, Brutus,' in that rich, hoarse voice with its overtones of good living. Instead he had to content himself with a ghostly glower, while Brutus swallowed and answered himself and carried on, somehow, without response. He had kept his head remarkably well, but long before he stammered that he would meet the shade at Philippi a great rustle had passed through the house. Ladies were recovering their voices. They screamed, and fainted in silk heaps all over the theatre. And the men, white and silent, or red and swearing, leaped to their feet and put their hands to the hilts of useless swords. The players, professional even in this extremity, attempted to continue, but the noise was so great that Ned Bellamy ordered the curtain to be rung down, and no calls were taken.

The *London Morning Penny Post* gave a highly-coloured and inaccurate account of Beaumont's Ghost, and speculated on the reason for his appearance. The old rivalry between Bellamy and Beaumont was raked up, with unfavourable accounts of brawls in taverns and an abortive duel in Leicester Fields. There was a timely reminder that Mrs Beaumont, as was, had become Mrs Bellamy less than a year after her first husband's death. The writer headed his article, 'Et tu, Brute', which many people considered to be an exquisite summing up of the situation.

Tom was too busy studying his next part, as Hamlet's father's ghost, to be concerned with the refinements of the *London Morning Penny Post*. This time he stopped the play in the first act instead of the last. One soldier fell from the battlements and broke his leg. Bellamy, as Hamlet, suffered a mild heart attack and was abed for six weeks with ten leeches. And the spectators fled from the theatre, bruising an orange girl in the process.

Ned returned as Macbeth, resolved to sit Tom's persecution out. He had warned his company and the public that the late Mr Beaumont might appear as Banquo's ghost, and to a certain degree they were prepared for this enormity. The attendance was excellent; and a Duchess, who should have been at home, almost produced the heir to a great estate in a White's Theatre box.

But Mr Mills did very well as Banquo and his ghost, without Tom's aid, and the feast passed off as an anti-climax. What no one expected was a bravura display over the witches' cauldron. With a versatility truly amazing to behold, Tom impersonated an Armed Head, a Bloody Child, A Child Crowned with a Tree in his Hand, a Show of Eight Kings and – having previously tripped Mr Mills up with a ghostly spear in the corridor – Banquo's Ghost. More fascinated than afraid, the audience watched every move, and then burst into sincere applause. A spirit Tom certainly was, but it was the spirit of a great actor and a true professional, and they rose out of their seats to honour him. He disappeared on a bow, and the play proceeded in peace.

Ned Bellamy, shrewd and courageous, measured his haunter even as he spoke his final lines. He knew that Sarah, good-natured and indolent in her mantle of fat, did not possess the fibre to confront Tom. But he knew that he must conquer or appease him, or lose the theatre and his livelihood. Ned had not missed the sudden pleasure on that ghostly florid face when the spectators stood in his honour, and he respected the ingenuity that Tom had put into the performance. So, as they took curtain after curtain, and the Duchess was carried out groaning, Ned reached a conclusion. He walked forward to where the wicks floated in an iron trough and held out his arms for silence.

'We have been honoured this evening by the presence of one well-known to us,' he said. 'And therefore, my lords, ladies and gentlemen, we shall leave the stage empty for a few moments, and I pray you give a token of your affection and esteem to the late great Mr Thomas Beaumont.'

Then he strode, heart beating too fast for his good or its own, into the wings. The audience, all fears exorcised, clapped and stamped and waved their handkerchiefs. The stage remained deserted by everything but three dusty bushes – which represented the Plain before the Castle – and the shadows thrown by the gently swinging candelabras in the roof. Then, very gradually, a stout gentleman with bright black eyes became visible, bowing and making a handsome leg. One hand spread affectedly across his lace cravat, the other wagged out of vanity behind his brocade coat. For fully a minute he accepted their plaudits. Then, just before he vanished, he looked directly at Ned Bellamy in a bewilderment of anger and gratitude. And Ned bowed very deeply and gravely, and said, 'Your servant, sir!'

His sting drawn, as it were, Tom became a part-time member of the company. Ned let it be known that, though there was no guarantee, the late Mr Beaumont might well appear – either as himself or someone else – at any time. And his virtuoso performance in *Richard III* was long remembered, when he appeared in quick succession as the ghosts of Prince Edward, King Henry VI, Clarence, Rivers, Grey and Vaughan, Hastings, the two young Princes, Lady Anne, and Buckingham – enough to disturb the sleep of any monarch. Sometimes he was observed standing a little shyly on the edge of the company, in a play which could not absorb his peculiar talents, and then Ned kindly summoned everyone from the stage, and the audience gave Tom Beaumont a special hand. And White's Theatre entered upon a decade of popularity, which was later attributed by historians to the quality of management, since they could hardly subscribe to the drawing power of a ghost.

Fire demolished White's in the latter part of the eighteenth century. Ned Bellamy died of a heart attack, attempting to fight flames beyond any man's control – even when that man is a desperate lover, resolved to rescue his lady. Gossip and malicious rumour said that Tom Beaumont started the fire in one of the tiring rooms, and was seen laughing in the ruins as his rival died. The *London Morning Penny Post* embroidered this story to such an extent that *The Gentleman's Magazine* felt bound to contradict it. There were witnesses to the event, they said, who saw Mr Beaumont appear at Mr Bellamy's side and attempt to pick up the bucket that fell from his hand. And many persons had seen him sitting in the ruins, like some masculine Niobe, weeping for his double loss.

Tom was lonely when Ned went, and vexed when Sarah followed him. And as the new theatre façade went up, and a new manager founded a new company, Tom discovered himself cherishing even such slight acquaintances as Mr Mills; simply because he had tripped him up with a ghostly spear, and borrowed his part for a few minutes. The new White's Theatre was grander and less lovable than the old one. An air of fighting gloriously against all odds had gone with the fire. White's was established now, prosperous, and far less exciting.

The new century, too, seemed to have sacrificed grace for bustle. As the industrial revolution became a reality instead of a threat, as the industrious Victorians replaced the elegant

Georgians, Tom became a displaced ghost. He sulked at his changed world, and pondered his exclusive position, for no one joined him. He had thought they would form a ghostly company, and continue in death as in life – only minus the inconveniences of life. But one by one his friends and colleagues left him; and when the humdrum soul of Mr Mills twanged straight to its Maker, Tom wept.

He had not the heart, if such an expression is permitted, to make a public appearance before 1840. By accident, he chose to materialise in the royal box when Her Majesty Queen Victoria was enjoying an evening at White's. Fortunately she was not disturbed, since two ushers attempted to turn him quietly out – and Tom, unused to such treatment, vanished in a huff. Later, glowering round a corner he overheard them talking.

'It wasn't real, my dear fellow. My hand went straight through its shoulder. Have they got a ghost here, do you imagine?'

The usher was very young, no great lover of the theatre proper, and no historian.

'It couldn't have been anyone of consequence,' he said, 'or I should have recognised him.'

Blighted, Tom sat alone in the empty theatre for a long time. He had thought that this life-in-death, monotonous though it often was, would go on unchanged for ever. But nothing remains the same, even for a walking shadow, and Tom Beaumont, as actor-manager and ghost, was forgotten.

The Theatre, once a dream of white and gold, was painted like a whore in the second half of the nineteenth century, christened 'White's Follies', and given over to Music Hall capers. Tom had no experience of this new medium, and no opportunity – since his haunting was limited – of comparing one Music Hall with another. But he recognised the second-rate when he saw it, and his pride suffered. In one or two of the players he felt there was something like promise, and when the audiences felt the same he was relieved and flattered. But he also noticed that if an actor or actress reached a certain standard of excellence they disappeared elsewhere, leaving him to contemplate performing dogs, and comedians with red noses.

A second fire, at which Tom did not assist with the water buckets, ravaged 'White's Follies'. He stood there gravely, hands behind his brocade coat, wig set aright, and contemplated the blaze with infinite satisfaction. Since he could not have his old building he preferred rubble. Spirits, as well as human beings, have their miseries and glories. The great difference is the time factor. So most of the nineteenth century had passed as wretchedly for Tom as, say, a decade would have dragged along in true life. He had grown accustomed to being ignored and unknown. He had survived the loss of his era and his contemporaries and the theatre as he once knew it. And he had learned to wait, to be passive. So he raised himself quite jauntily on his heels, and craned his neck to observe a great beam crumble and fall in a shower of sparks. He was extremely interested in the new fire-fighting contraptions: the scarlet and brass monster, bell ringing, hurtling through the streets; the men in strange uniforms and shining helmets; the yards of rubber hose and jets of water. It was the best evening he had had in the last fifty years. If only he had been able, a lady on each arm, to celebrate the event at a tavern afterwards – the oysters, the wine, the company.

A group of City gentlemen, rich in pocket and reverent of theatre history, re-built White's under its former name. A new management attempted to devote itself to the presentation of Restoration Drama. They found it expedient, however, to intersperse this with popular comedy; and at last specialised in light fare, with an occasional Restoration piece thrown in for good measure.

Tom, ever adaptable, took part when he could. But a ghost, generally speaking, is as noticeable as his audience makes him; and Tom was either overlooked or accepted as a genuine member of the crowd scenes. The nineteen twenties were upon him, and down he went in a flood of cigarette holders, long beads, short skirts, and general scepticism. Sullenly, he walked through scenery to keep in practice. Unnoticed, he appeared in dressing rooms, to be put down as an excess of lobster or alcohol. Pettishly, he refused to materialise at all – and was never missed.

In the thirties the theatre was converted into a cinema, round which he wandered in total bewilderment. A shadow himself, he could not understand the shadows on the screen. Real from a distance, they became unsubstantial at close range. He must have vanished through the glowing screen a thousand times in an effort to find them. But what changes of character, costume and country! What landscapes and seascapes, what drawing room scenes, what minute detail! He marvelled at the ingenuity, walked closer to touch or inspect some specially fine article of furniture or china – and found nothing. Later, he stood behind the projector and watched the operator spin his reels of magic. And when the lights were out and the house empty he sat for hours, contemplating this new phenomenon. Then he rose and sighed, brushed imaginary dust from his breeches and set his wig aright, and said aloud, 'Damme! What a princely spectacle I should have made of *Macbeth* with this moving theatre. Why, sir,' though no companion was there to hear him, 'I could have put on a battle scene such as would have the ladies in a faint, and the gentlemen reaching for their swords!'

In time he became a connoisseur of this new medium; separating the good from the indifferent, and nourishing a particular fondness for Marlene Dietrich. He later added Rita Hayworth and Marilyn Monroe to his list of favourites.

The cinema queues waned, drawn away by yet another innovation of which Tom was ignorant: the television. He had not been a manager, alive and dead, for two centuries, without sensing financial disaster. In sorrow he counted the empty seats, and clicked his tongue and shook his head. Unsurprised, he watched the programmes become desperately popular without effect. And when the doors finally closed he mourned this latest passing.

Decorators arrived, sharpening his interest briefly, but they brought no glad tidings. The cinema became a Bingo Hall. It took Tom only three weeks to decide that this was not his métier, and then he acted. His appearance from the shadows, foppishly dressed and with one wrathful arm extended, caused great consternation. And lest anyone should think they had been mistaken he appeared nightly, in the same place and in the same attitude. The Hall was shut at the end of his first week's performance, for repairs the management said. Tom knew better, and slapped his thighs and laughed until his shoulders and belly shook. Then he waited for the next move.

It came in the homely shape of a medium, whom the manager escorted to the theatre the following Sunday, in a mixture of urgency and embarrassment.

Tom surveyed her with contemptuous interest, being a sexual snob; and wondered afresh why any women chose to live after losing her physical attractions. But Mrs Rout had interests other than the pleasure of the opposite sex, and snuffed the air in much the same fashion as a retriever snuffs game.

'There's something here,' she announced, rubbing her hands and smiling. 'Oh, my word, yes. Very strong. Very strong. You did well to call me in.'

Then she requested absolute silence, sat down with her hands pressed over her eyes, and concentrated. For the first time in two hundred years or so, Tom was aware of communication, though no word was spoken. And he stood up, brought to judgement. But his first words were as arrogant as ever.

'Madam,' he said. 'I should be monstrous obliged if you would take your leave of me!'

'I want to help you,' purred Mrs Rout, intent upon her own purposes. 'I can give you peace and rest.'

'Madam,' said Tom irritably, 'I have had enough rest to content any man living or dead – and I never asked for peace. But, Madam, if you have any influence with the present management I do beg you to impart this message. Tell them, if you please, that I shall continue to appear nightly until some form of genuine theatre returns to this unhappy building!'

The medium moaned and held her neck.

'Ah! You have had a constriction here,' she cried. 'I feel it.

You died of a constriction!' Her imagination leaped ahead of her. 'Choking, choking. Now I see it all. You hanged yourself in a dressing room – the aura was very strong there when I came in.'

'Pox on you, madam,' said Tom rudely. 'I died on a rotten oyster!'

'Should we fetch a clergyman, Mrs Rout?' the manager whispered. 'And then the poor – soul – could be exorcised.'

'God's teeth, sir,' cried Tom. 'No clergyman shall meddle with me, alive or dead!'

'Poor wandering spirit,' said Mrs Rout, absorbed in her own misguided sympathy. 'You shall have *rest*. You *shall* have rest.'

In vain Tom swore at her, shook her shoulder, kicked the manager, and shouted imprecations at the top of his ghostly voice. The medium suddenly came to, sneezed, smiled, reached for her handbag, and requested to be taken forthwith back to Balham.

On Tuesday night the exorcism took place, with a discretion and thoroughness truly admirable. In a matter of minutes Tom felt as though his feet had been untethered. He bobbed up to the ceiling, in a positive fusillade of oaths, and soared out into the evening sky – leaving those below to congratulate themselves and him on his freedom.

In rage and terror he floated over London, catching at chimney pots, at spires, at weathercocks and steeples, until an arm as insubstantial as his own arrested him.

'Ned Bellamy!' said Tom, amazed. And then sternly, to cover his delight, he cried: 'Well sir, you have been long enough looking up an old acquaintance!'

'Why Tom, the fault is of your own making. You *would* stay, sir.'

Tom took a slow turn round St Paul's dome and came to rest, clinging to Ned's ruffles.

'*I* would stay, sir?' he cried indignantly.

'Aye sir, and *shall* stay if you wish. Though I promise you we are all very well in another place.'

'Have I a choice, then, Ned?' Tom asked.

The nod astonished him, and his brows contracted as he thought.

'Ned,' he said wistfully. 'I should like to stay just a while longer. Ned! Do not go for a moment, I pray you! I am like a damned pigeon wheeling when you take away your arm. I am not yet used to the motion. Ned, I have all manner of things to tell you. They have moving theatres, Ned, that live in round boxes and are shone onto a screen. And the players now are something different from our own.'

'Vanity, Tom, all vanity. I could tell you of things so fine that you could never imagine them. Vanity, Tom.'

The little black eyes twinkled. One splendid hand brushed a speck of ghostly dust from the ghostly cravat.

'Ah, but Ned,' said Tom slyly, 'I was always a vain man! A little while longer, Ned. A mere century or so. What difference can that make to my eternity? Just to see, Ned. Just to watch. But you will ask me again?' he added, with some anxiety.

'Aye, Tom. Go your ways! And take care while you find your legs again. These steeples are the very devil for a middle-aged ghost on a dark night!'

Like one released from prison, Tom Beaumont floated and peered and pondered. Unrestricted by White's Theatre, he was seeking employment, and had all the leisure in the world with which to find it.

There is a new travelling theatre company in the United States of America, who specialise in Shakespearian plays. At first they had a hard thin time of it, but their fame is growing and they expect to tour Europe this winter. The company do not encourage the questions and attentions of the Press, which gives them the finest publicity available because of this peculiar reticence.

They have their idiosyncrasies, such as producing all their plays in eighteenth-century costume. But their particular genius lies in illusion and effect. I think that of all their productions I would recommend *Macbeth*. The spectacle over the witches' cauldron is truly astonishing for its versatility. Though I *have* heard critics express a preference for *Richard III*, when no less than eleven ghosts in quick succession chill the blood, and send a murmur of admiration and terror through the house. And I must admit that I have never seen Hamlet's father's ghost so well portrayed; while the sight of Caesar's helmeted shade, striding the bloody battlefield at Philippi, would bring a clutch of horror to the stoutest heart.

XII

Mrs Lunt

Hugh Walpole

'Do you believe in ghosts?' I asked Runciman. I had to ask him this very platitudinous question more because he was so difficult a man to spend an hour with rather than for any other reason. You know his books, perhaps, or more probably you don't know them – *The Running Man*, *The Elm Tree*, and *Crystal and Candlelight*. He is one of those little men who are constant enough in this age of immense overproduction of books, men who publish every autumn their novel, who arouse by that publication in certain critics eager appreciation and praise, who have a small and faithful public, whose circulation is very small indeed, who, when you meet them, have little to say, are often shy and nervous, pessimistic and remote from daily life. Such men do fine work, are made but little of in their own day, and perhaps fifty years after their death are rediscovered by some digging critic and become a sort of cult with a new generation.

I asked Runciman that question because, for some unknown reason, I had invited him to dinner at my flat, and was now faced with a long evening filled with that most tiresome of all conversations, talk that dies every two minutes and has to be revived with terrific exertions. Being myself a critic, and having on many occasions praised Runciman's work, he was the more nervous and shy with me; had I abused it, he would perhaps have had plenty to say – he was that kind of man. But my question was a lucky one: it roused him instantly, his long, bony body became full of a new energy, his eyes stared into a rich and exciting reminiscence, he spoke without pause, and I took care not to interrupt him. He certainly told me one of the most astounding stories I have ever heard. Whether it was true or not I cannot, of course, say. These ghost stories are nearly always at second or third hand. I had, at any rate, the good fortune to secure mine from the source. Moreover, Runciman was not a liar; he was too serious for that. He himself admitted that he was not sure, at this distance of time, as to whether the thing had gained as the years passed. However, here it is as he told it.

'It was some fifteen years ago,' he said. 'I went down to Cornwall to stay with Robert Lunt. Do you remember his name? No, I suppose you do not. He wrote several novels; some of those half-and-half things that are not quite novels, not quite poems, rather mystical and picturesque, and are the very devil to do well. De la Mare's *Return* is a good example of the kind of thing. I had reviewed somewhere his last book, and reviewed it favourably, and received from him a really touching letter showing that the man was thirsting for praise, and also, I fancied, for company. He lived in Cornwall somewhere on the sea-coast, and his wife had died some two years before; he said he was quite alone there, and would I come and spend Christmas with him; he hoped I would not think this impertinent; he expected that I would be engaged already, but he could not resist the chance. Well, I wasn't engaged; far from it. If Lunt was lonely, so was I; if Lunt was a failure, so was I; I was touched, as I have said, by his letter, and I accepted his invitation. As I went down in the train to Penzance I wondered what kind of a man he would be. I had never seen any photographs of him; he was not the sort of author whose picture the newspapers publish. He must be, I fancied, about my own age – perhaps rather older. I know when we're lonely how some of us are for ever imagining that a friend will somewhere turn up, that ideal friend who will understand all one's feelings, who will give one affection without being sentimental, who will take an interest in one's affairs without being impertinent – yes, the sort of friend one never finds.

'I fancy that I became quite romantic about Lunt before I reached Penzance. We would talk, he and I, about all those literary questions that seemed to me at that time so absorbing; we would perhaps often stay together and even travel abroad on those little journeys that are so swiftly melancholy when one is alone, so delightful when one has a perfect companion. I imagined him as sparse and delicate and refined, with a sort of wistfulness and rather childish play of fancy. We had both, so far, failed in our careers, but perhaps together we would do great things.

'When I arrived at Penzance it was almost dark, and the snow, threatened all day by an overhanging sky, had begun gently and timorously to fall. He had told me in his letter that a fly would be at the station to take me to his house; and there I found it – a funny old weather-beaten carriage with a funny old weather-beaten driver. At this distance of time my imagination may have created many things, but I fancy that from the moment I was shut into that carriage some dim suggestion of fear and apprehension attacked me. I fancy that I had some absurd impulse to get out of the thing and take the night train back to London again – an action that would have been very unlike me, as I had always a sort of obstinate determination to carry through anything that I had begun. In any case, I was uncomfortable in that carriage; it had, I remember, a nasty, musty smell of damp straw and stale eggs, and it seemed to confine me so closely as though it were determined that, once I was in, I should never get out again. Then, it was bitterly cold; I was colder during that drive than I have ever been before or since. It was that penetrating cold that seems to pierce your very brain, so that I could not think with any clearness, but only wish again and again that I hadn't come. Of course, I could see nothing – only feel the jolt over the uneven road – and once and again we seemed to fight our way through dark paths, because I could feel the overhanging branches of the trees knock against the cab with mysterious taps, as though they were trying to give me some urgent message.

'Well, I mustn't make more of it than the facts allow, and I mustn't see into it all the significance of the events that followed. I only know that as the drive proceeded I became more and more miserable: miserable with the cold of my body, the misgivings of my imagination, the general loneliness of my case.

'At last we stopped. The old scarecrow got slowly off his box, with many heavings and sighings, came to the cab door and, with great difficulty and irritating slowness, opened it. I got out of it, and found that the snow was now falling very heavily indeed, and that the path was lightened with its soft, mysterious glow. Before me was a humped and ungainly shadow: the house that was to receive me. I could make nothing of it in that darkness, but only stood there shivering while the old man pulled at the door-bell with a sort of frantic energy as though he were anxious to be rid of the whole job as quickly as possible and return to his own place. At last, after what seemed an endless time, the door opened, and an old man, who might have been own brother to the driver, poked out his head. The two old men talked together, and at last my bag was shouldered and I was permitted to come in out of the piercing cold.

'Now this, I know, is not imagination. I have never at any period of my life hated at first sight so vigorously any dwelling-place into which I have ever entered as I did that house. There was nothing especially disagreeable about my first vision of the hall. It was a large, dark place, lit by two dim lamps, cold and cheerless; but I got no particular impression of it because at once I was conducted out of it, led along a passage, and then introduced into a room which was, I saw at once, as warm and comfortable as the hall had been dark and dismal. I was, in fact, so eagerly pleased at the large and leaping fire that I moved towards it at once, not noting, at the first moment, the presence of my host; and when I did see him I could not believe that it was he. I have told you the kind of man that I had expected; but, instead of the sparse, sensitive artist, I found facing me a large, burly man, over six foot, I should fancy, as broad-shouldered as he was tall, giving evidence of great muscular strength, the lower part of his face hidden by a black, pointed beard.

'But if I was astonished at the sight of him, I was doubly

amazed when he spoke. His voice was thin and piping, like that of some old woman, and the little nervous gestures that he made with his hands were even more feminine than his voice. But I had to allow, perhaps, for excitement, for excited he was; he came up to me, took my hand in both of his, and held it as though he would never let it go. In the evening, when we sat over our port, he apologized for this. "I was so glad to see you," he said, "I couldn't believe that really you would come; you are the first visitor of my own kind that I have had here for ever so long. I was ashamed, indeed, of asking you, but I had to snatch at the chance – it means too much to me."

'His eagerness, in fact, had something disturbing about it; something pathetic, too. He simply couldn't do too much for me: he led me through funny crumbling old passages, the boards creaking under us at every step, up some dark stairs, the walls hung, so far as I could see in the dim light, with faded yellow photographs of places, and showed me into my room with a deprecating agitated gesture as though he expected me at the first sight of it to turn and run. I didn't like it any more than I liked the rest of the house; but that was not my host's fault. He had done everything he possibly could for me: there was a large fire flaming in the open fireplace, there was a hot bottle, as he explained to me, in the big four-poster bed, and the old man who had opened the door to me was already taking my clothes out of my bag and putting them away. Lunt's nervousness was almost sentimental. He put both his hands on my shoulders and said, looking at me pleadingly. "If you only knew what it is for me to have you here, the talks we'll have. Well, well, I must leave you. You'll come down and join me, won't you, as soon as you can?"

'It was then, when I was left alone in my room, that I had my second impulse to flee. Four candles in tall old silver candlesticks were burning brightly, and these, with the blazing fire, gave plenty of light; and yet the room was in some way dim, as though a faint smoke pervaded it, and I remember that I went to one of the old lattice windows and threw it open for a moment as though I felt stifled. Two things quickly made me close it. One was the intense cold which, with a fluttering scamper of snow, blew into the room; the other was the quite deafening roar of the sea, which seemed to fling itself at my very face as though it wanted to knock me down. I quickly shut the window, turned round, and saw an old woman standing just inside the door. Now every story of this kind depends for its interest on its verisimilitude. Of course, to make my tale convincing I should be able to prove to you that I saw that old woman; but I can't. I can only urge upon you my rather dreary reputation of probity. You know that I'm a teetotaller, and always have been, and, most important evidence of all, I was not expecting to see an old woman; and yet I hadn't the least doubt in the world but that it was an old woman I saw. You may talk about shadows, clothes hanging on the back of the door, and the rest of it. I don't know. I've no theories about this story; I'm not a spiritualist, I don't know that I believe in anything especially, except the beauty of beautiful things.

'We'll put it, if you like, that I fancied that I saw an old woman, and my fancy was so strong that I can give you to this day a pretty detailed account of her appearance. She wore a black silk dress and on her breast was a large, ugly gold brooch; she had black hair, brushed back from her forehead and parted down the middle; she wore a collar of some white stuff round her throat; her face was one of the wickedest, most malignant, and furtive that I have ever seen – very white in colour. She was shrivelled enough now, but might once have been rather beautiful. She stood there quietly, her hands at her side. I thought that she was some kind of housekeeper. "I have everything I want, thank you," I said. "What a splendid fire!" I turned for a moment towards it, and when I looked back she was gone. I thought nothing of this, of course, but drew up an old chair covered with green faded tapestry, and thought that I would read a little from some book that I had brought down with me before I went to join my host. The fact was that I was not very intent upon joining him before I must. I didn't like him. I had already made up my mind that I would find some excuse to return to London as soon as possible. I can't tell you why I didn't like him, except that I was myself very reserved and had, like many Englishmen, a great distrust of demonstrations, especially from another man. I hadn't cared for the way in which he had put his hands on my shoulders, and I felt perhaps that I wouldn't be able to live up to all his eager excitement about me.

'I sat in my chair and took up my book, but I had not been reading for more than two minutes before I was conscious of a most unpleasant smell. Now, there are all sorts of smells – healthy and otherwise – but I think the nastiest is that chilly kind of odour that comes from bad sanitation and stuffy rooms combined; you meet it sometimes at little country inns and decrepit town lodgings. This smell was so definite that I could almost locate it; it came from near the door. I got up, approached the door, and at once it was as though I were drawing near to somebody who, if you'll forgive the impoliteness, was not accustomed to taking too many baths. I drew back just as I might had an actual person been there. Then quite suddenly the smell was gone, the room was fresh, and I saw, to my surprise, that one of the windows had opened and that snow was again blowing in. I closed it and went downstairs.

'The evening that followed was odd enough. My host was not in himself an unlikeable man; he did his very utmost to please me. He had a fine culture and a wide knowledge of books and things. He became quite cheerful as the evening went on; gave me a good dinner in a funny little old dining-room hung with some admirable mezzotints. The old serving man looked after us – a funny old man, with a long white beard like a goat – and, oddly enough, it was from him that I first recaught my earlier apprehension. He had just put the dessert on the table, had arranged my plate in front of me, when I saw him give a start and look towards the door. My attention was attracted to this because his hand, as it touched the plate, suddenly trembled. My eyes followed, but I could see nothing. That he was frightened of something was perfectly clear, and then (it may, of course, very easily have been fancy) I thought that I detected once more that strange unwholesome smell.

'I forgot this again when we were both seated in front of a splendid fire in the library. Lunt had a very fine collection of books, and it was delightful to him, as it is to every book-collector, to have somebody with him who could really appreciate them. We stood looking at one book after another and talking eagerly about some of the minor early English novelists who were my especial hobby – Bage, Godwin, Henry Mackenzie, Mrs Shelley, Mat Lewis, and others – when once again he affected me most unpleasantly by putting his arm round my shoulders. I have all my life disliked intensely to be touched by certain people. I suppose we all feel like this. It is one of those inexplicable things; and I disliked this so much that I abruptly drew away.

'Instantly he was changed into a man of furious and ungovernable rage; I thought that he was going to strike me. He stood there quivering all over, the words pouring out of his mouth incoherently, as though he were mad and did not know what he was saying. He accused me of insulting him, of abusing his hospitality, of throwing his kindness back into his face, and of a thousand other ridiculous things; and I can't tell you how strange it was to hear all this coming out in that shrill piping voice as though it were from an agitated woman, and yet to see with one's eyes that big, muscular frame, those immense shoulders, and that dark bearded face.

'I said nothing. I am, physically, a coward. I dislike, above anything else in the world, any sort of quarrel. At last I brought out, "I am very sorry. I didn't mean anything. Please forgive me," and then hurriedly turned to leave the room. At once he changed again; now he was almost in tears. He implored me not to go; said it was his wretched temper, but that he was so miserable and unhappy, and had for so long now been alone and desolate that he hardly knew what he was doing. He begged me to give him another chance, and if I would only listen to his story I would perhaps be more patient with him.

'At once, so oddly is man constituted, I changed in my feelings towards him. I was very sorry for him. I saw that he was a man on the edge of his nerves, and that he really did need some help and sympathy, and would be quite distracted if he could not get it. I put my hand on his shoulder to quieten him and to show him that I bore no malice, and I felt that his great body was quivering from head to foot. We sat down again, and in an odd, rambling manner he told me his story. It amounted to very little, and the gist of it was that, rather to have some sort of companionship than from any impulse of passion, he had married, some fifteen years before, the daughter of a neighbouring clergyman. They had had no very happy life together, and at the last, he told me quite frankly, he had hated her. She had been mean, overbearing, and narrow-minded; it had been, he confessed, nothing but a relief to him when, just a year ago, she had suddenly died from heart failure. He had thought then that things would go better with him, but they had not; nothing had gone right with him since. He hadn't been able to work, many of his friends had ceased to come to see him, he had found it even difficult to get servants to stay with him, he was desperately lonely, he slept badly – that was why his temper was so terribly on edge.

'He had no one in the house with him save the old man, who was, fortunately, an excellent cook, and a boy – the old man's grandson. "Oh, I thought," I said, "that that excellent meal to-night was cooked by your housekeeper." "My housekeeper?" he answered. "There's no woman in the house." "Oh, but one came to my room," I replied, "this evening – an old lady-like looking person in a black silk dress." "You were mistaken," he answered in the oddest voice, as though he were exerting all the strength that he possessed to keep himself quiet and controlled. "I am sure that I saw her," I answered. "There couldn't be any mistake." And I described her to him. "You were mistaken," he repeated again. "Don't you see that you must have been when I tell you there is no woman in the house?" I reassured him quickly lest there should be another outbreak of rage. Then there followed the oddest kind of appeal. Urgently, as though his very life depended upon it, he begged me to stay with him for a few days. He implied, although he said nothing definitely, that he was in great trouble, that if only I would stay for a few days all would be well, that if ever in all my life I had had a chance of doing a kind action I had one now, that he couldn't expect me to stop in so dreary a place, but that he would never forget it if I did. He spoke in a voice of such urgent distress that I reassured him as I might a child, promising that I would stay, and shaking hands with him on it as though it were a kind of solemn oath between us.

II

'I am sure that you would wish me to give you this incident as it occurred, and if the final catastrophe seems to come, as it were, accidentally, I can only say to you that that was how it happened. It is since the event that I have tried to put two and two together, and that they don't altogether make four is the fault that mine shares, I suppose, with every true ghost story.

'But the truth is that after that very strange episode between us I had a very good night. I slept the sleep of all justice, cosy and warm, in my four-poster, with the murmur of the sea beyond the windows to rock my slumbers. Next morning, too, was bright and cheerful, the sun sparkling down on the snow, and the snow sparkling back to the sun as though they were glad to see one another. I had a very pleasant morning looking at Lunt's books, talking to him, and writing one or two letters. I must say that, after all, I liked the man. His appeal to me on the night before had touched me. So few people, you see, had ever appealed to me about anything. His nervousness was there and the constant sense of apprehension, yet he seemed to be putting the best face on it, doing his utmost to set me at my ease in order to induce me to stay, I suppose, and to give him a little of that company that he so terribly needed. I dare say if I had not been so busy about the books I would not have been so happy. There was a strange eerie silence about that house if one ever stopped to listen; and once, I remember, sitting at the old bureau writing a letter, I raised my head and looked up, and caught Lunt watching as though he wondered whether I had heard or noticed anything. And so I listened too, and it seemed to me as though someone were on the other side of the library door with their hand raised to knock; a quaint notion, with nothing to support it, but I could have sworn that if I had gone to the door and opened it suddenly someone would have been there.

'However, I was cheerful enough, and after lunch quite happy. Lunt asked me if I would like a walk, and I said I would; and we started out in the sunshine over the crunching snow towards the sea. I don't remember of what we talked; we seemed to be now quite at our ease with one another. We crossed the fields to a certain point, looked down at the sea – smooth now, like silk – and turned back. I remember that I was so cheerful that I seemed suddenly to take a happy view of all my prospects. I began to confide in Lunt, telling him of my little plans, of my hopes for the book that I was then writing, and even began rather timidly to suggest to him that perhaps we should do something together; that what we both needed was a friend of common taste with ourselves. I know that I was talking on, that we had crossed a little village street, and were turning up the path towards the dark avenue of trees that led to his house, when suddenly the change came.

'What I first noticed was that he was not listening to me; his gaze was fixed beyond me, into the very heart of the black clump of trees that fringed the silver landscape. I looked too, and my heart bounded. There, standing just in front of the trees, as though she were waiting for us, was the old woman whom I had seen in my room the night before. I stopped. "Why, there she is!" I said. "That's the old woman of whom I was speaking – the old woman who came to my room." He caught my shoulder with his hand. "There's nothing there," he said. "Don't you see that that's shadow? What's the matter with you? Can't you see that there's nothing?" I stepped forward, and there was nothing, and I wouldn't, to this day, be able to tell you whether it was hallucination or not. I can only say that, from that moment, the afternoon appeared to become dark.

'As we entered into the avenue of trees, silently and hurrying as though someone were behind us, the dusk seemed to have fallen so that I could scarcely see my way. We reached the house breathless. He hastened into his study as though I were not with him, but I followed and, closing the door behind me, said, with all the force that I had at command: "Now, what is this? What is it that's troubling you? You must tell me! How can I help you if you don't?" And he replied, in so strange a voice that it was as though he had gone out of his mind: "I tell you there's nothing! Can't you believe me when I tell you there's nothing at all? I'm quite all right ... Oh, my God! – my God! ... don't leave me! ... This is the very day – the very night she said ... But I did nothing, I tell you – I did nothing – it's only her beastly malice ... " He broke off. He still held my arm with his hand. He made strange movements, wiping his forehead as though it were damp with sweat, almost pleading with me; then suddenly angry again, then beseeching once more, as though I had refused him the one thing he wanted.

'I saw that he was truly not far from madness, and I began myself to have a sudden terror of this damp, dark house, this great, trembling man, and something more that was worse than they. But I pitied him. How could you or any man have helped it? I made him sit down in the armchair beside the fire, which had now dwindled to a few glimmering red coals. I let him hold me close to him with his arm and clutch my hand with his, and I repeated, as quiet as I might: "But tell me; don't be afraid, whatever it is you have done. Tell me what danger it is you fear, and then we can face it together." "Fear! fear!" he repeated; and then, with a mighty effort which I could not but admire, he summoned all his control. "I'm off my head," he said, "with loneliness and depression. My wife died a year ago on this very night. We hated one another. I couldn't be sorry when she died, and she knew it. When that last heart attack came on, between her gasps she told me that she would return, and I've always dreaded this night. That's partly why I asked you to come, to have anyone here, anybody, and you've been very kind – more kind than I had any right to expect. You must think me insane going on like this, but see me through to-night and we'll have splendid times together. Don't desert me now – now, of all times!" I promised that I would not. I soothed him as best I could. We sat there, for I know not how long, through the gathering dark; we neither of us moved, the fire died out, and the room was lit with a strange dim glow that came from the snowy landscape beyond the uncurtained windows. Ridiculous, perhaps, as I look back at it. We sat there, I in a chair close to his, hand in hand, like a couple of lovers; but, in real truth, two men terrified, fearful of what was coming, and unable to do anything to meet it.

'I think that that was perhaps the strangest part of it; a sort of paralysis that crept over me. What would you or anyone else have done – summoned the old man, gone down to the village inn, fetched the local doctor? I could do nothing but see the snow-shine move like trembling water about the furniture and hear, through the urgent silence, the faint hoot of an owl from the trees in the wood.

III

'Oddly enough, I can remember nothing, try as I may, between that strange vigil and the moment when I myself, wakened out of a brief sleep, sat up in bed to see Lunt standing inside my room holding a candle. He was wearing a nightshirt, and looked huge in the candlelight, his black beard falling intensely dark on the white stuff of his shirt. He came very quietly towards my bed, the candle throwing flickering shadows about the room. When he spoke it was in a voice low and subdued, almost a whisper. "Would you come," he asked, "only for half an hour – just for half an hour?" he repeated, staring at me as though he didn't know me. "I'm unhappy without somebody – very unhappy." Then he looked over his shoulder, held the candle high above his head, and stared piercingly at every part of the room. I could see that something had happened to him, that he had taken another step into the country of Fear – a step that had withdrawn him from me and from every other human being. He whispered: "When you come, tread softly; I don't want anyone to hear us." I did what I could. I got out of bed, put on my dressing-gown and slippers, and tried to persuade him to stay with me. The fire was almost dead, but I told him that we would build it up again, and that we would sit there and wait for the morning; but no, he repeated again and again: "It's better in my own room; we're safer there." "Safe from what?" I asked him, making him look at me. "Lunt, wake up! You're as though you were asleep. There's nothing to fear. We've nobody but ourselves. Stay here and let us talk, and have done with this nonsense." But he wouldn't answer; only drew me forward down the dark passage, and then turned into his room, beckoning me to follow. He got into bed and sat hunched up there, his hands holding his knees, staring at the door, and every once and again shivering with a little tremor. The only light in the room was that from the candle, now burning low, and the only sound was the purring whisper of the sea.

'It seemed to make little difference to him that I was there. He did not look at me, but only at the door, and when I spoke to him he did not answer me nor seem to hear what I had said. I sat down beside the bed and, in order to break the silence, talked on about anything, about nothing, and was dropping off, I think, into a confused doze, when I heard his voice breaking across mine. Very clearly and distinctly he said: "If I killed her, she deserved it; she was never a good wife to me, not from the first; she shouldn't have irritated me as she did – she knew what my temper was. She had a worse one than mine, though. She can't touch me; I'm as strong as she is." And it was then, as clearly as I can now remember, that his voice suddenly sank into a sort of gentle whisper, as though he were almost glad that his fears had been confirmed. He whispered: "She's there!" I cannot possibly describe to you how that whisper seemed to let Fear loose like water through my body. I could see nothing – the candle was flaming high in the last moment of its life – I could see nothing; but Lunt suddenly screamed, with a shrill cry like a tortured animal in agony: "Keep her off me, keep her away from me, keep her off – keep her off!" He caught me, his hands digging into my shoulders; then, with an awful effect of constricted muscles, as though rigor had caught and held him, his arms slowly fell away, he slipped back on to the bed as though someone were pushing him, his hands fell against the sheet, his whole body jerked with a convulsive effort, and then he rolled over. I saw nothing; only quite distinctly in my nostrils was that same fetid odour that I had known on the preceding evening. I rushed to the door, opened it, shouted down the long passage again and again, and soon the old man came running. I sent him for the doctor, and then could not return to the room, but stood there listening, hearing nothing save the whisper of the sea, the loud ticking of the hall clock. I flung open the window at the end of the passage; the sea rushed in with its precipitant roar; some bells chimed the hour. Then at last, beating into myself more courage, I turned back towards the room ...'

'Well?' I asked as Runciman paused. 'He was dead, of course?'

'Dead, the doctor afterwards said, of heart failure.'

'Well?' I asked again.

'That's all.' Runciman paused. 'I don't know whether you can even call it a ghost story. My idea of the old woman may have been all hallucination. I don't even know whether his wife was like that when she was alive. She may have been large and fat. Lunt died of an evil conscience.'

'Yes,' I said.

'The only thing,' Runciman added at last, after a long pause, 'is that on Lunt's body there were marks – on his neck especially, some on his chest – as of fingers pressing in, scratches and dull blue marks. He may, in his terror, have caught at his own throat ...'

'Yes,' I said again.

'Anyway' – Runciman shivered – 'I don't like Cornwall – beastly county. Queer things happen there – something in the air ...'

'So I've heard,' I answered. 'And now have a drink. We both will.'

XIII

The Anniversary

Denys Val Baker

Like to many strange, indeed, unforgettable evenings, this one began quite casually. I was on a motoring holiday in Cornwall with several friends, and we had spent a pleasant hour or two drinking in a quiet pub outside Penzance. At closing time, as we were unwilling to end such a beautiful summer evening so early, we decided to search for a country club which one of our party had been told of by a friend in London. 'Mind you,' he said, 'it's a long time since he was there – during the last war it was, when he was stationed down here. But he says it's a lovely old place. Somewhere near Land's End ... He told me the way.'

We piled into three cars, two larger ones filled with my friends, and my own two-seater, in which I brought up the rear, driving alone. Just in case we should lose touch, the man who knew about the club had told me: 'You can't go wrong; about eight miles along the road from Penzance, and then there are some big gates, and you'll see a large drive leading to the club. It's called The Silver Wings.'

It was an exhilarating journey along the lonely roads that headed towards Land's End. The air smelled sweet and fragrant, and though dusk had fallen, there was a curious phosphorescent light out of which hedges, walls and occasional buildings loomed in shapes of fantasy. I drove on and on, along interminably winding roads, one eye fixed on the red light of the car ahead, the cool summer night air ruffling my hair, my eyes fixed on that elusive red light.

Suddenly I realised that the red light had disappeared, that I was alone, somehow having lost track of my leader. It didn't seem to matter. It was such a lovely night; I remembered the instructions. And, sure enough, after a while I saw the huge stone gateways to a drive. I swung my car to the right, my headlights picked out the signs: 'The Silver Wings Club'.

I drove my car up a long drive, lined on either side by rhododendron bushes. I felt a strange excitement as the drive curved round, but even so, I was hardly prepared for the grandiose final sweep up to the massive porchway of what seemed to be a manor house in the great tradition: rambling, with big bay windows and ivy-covered walls, and even small turrets, whose outline I could make out against a moonlit sky. Behind the drawn curtains there were lights.

I was puzzled that I could not see my friends' cars, but as there were several rows, disappearing into shadows, I assumed they were somewhere in the darkness. I turned and walked over the gravel and up the steps. Perhaps it was the effect of the night air during the drive, but I felt very gay and carefree. I was reminded, curiously, of those wartime years when everything seemed on razor's edge, and one grabbed at the moment in defiance of whatever grim destiny lay ahead.

I pushed open the door and went into an impressive hallway, with dark panelled walls and a stone floor covered here and there with rugs. One or two oil paintings hung on the walls, portraits of ancient cavaliers and coquettish ladies, perhaps family heirlooms. But now this one-time family house was plainly given over to its new function, for I could hear quite clearly the murmur of voices raised in conversation and laughter. Pleased to have reached the end of my journey, I went through some swinging doors at one end of the hall.

Here, obviously, was the hub of the Silver Wings Club. It was a long, low room, with carpets as well as dark panelling, altogether more cosy than the hall. The air was thick with smoke. I could not see my friends. But this was hardly surprising, as there must have been fifty or sixty people in the room, standing around in groups. Quite a few of them, I noticed, were in RAF uniforms. Everyone seemed young and in high spirits. I felt curiously at home: not exactly that 'I-have-been-here-before' feeling, but, well, something like it.

Above all, I had a curious sensation of being at ease, of people who were making me feel welcome.

Indeed, a man at the bar beckoned to me and said heartily: 'My dear fellow, have a drink on me.'

I smiled. 'But I don't really know you.'

'That doesn't matter, old boy. All friends here. What'll it be?'

I accepted his offer of a whisky and stood leaning against the bar, surveying the scene. Over in one corner a group were playing bar billiards, in another a large circle talked animatedly – at the far end of the room couples were dancing to the tinkling sound of a rather decrepit old piano. I had to admit that the girls seemed all good-looking, and yet – and yet there was something about them that slightly bothered me, something a little unfamiliar. I studied one of them closely. Wasn't there something unusual about her hair, her dress, her general style ...? Yes, I decided, in some curious way the girls seemed to be dressed in an old-fashioned way. That was it! But somehow, in such a setting, it did not matter. What mattered was the air of gaiety, of happiness, of everyone having a good time.

Indeed, as the evening grew livelier and livelier, it began to dawn on me that there was about it a sense not so much of abandon, as of – desperation; as if, in some way, these people had an awareness of time and its limitations. A curious thought, I reflected, and I attempted to rid myself of it. Yet it came back to me again and again, as gradually I became enveloped by the celebrations, joining in groups, drinking to people's health, dancing, toasting, laughing. Several times I caught remarks from men in uniform: 'Off duty tonight?' and 'I've a thirty-six-hour-pass.' I guessed there must be an Air Force Station near.

As it got later, we seemed to gather in a circle around the piano. The young man playing was good-looking, with fair hair and a moustache. He held his head up as he played and hummed the tunes, and soon a lot of us were singing. Something about the tunes, like the women's dresses, seemed again a little unfamiliar. And yet there could be no doubt that the men in the club knew every word of the tunes. For that matter, so did I, really – only it was some time since I had heard them.

It was a strange and wonderful experience, standing in close comradeship with the others, while the smoky air got thicker and thicker, singing to the tinkling sound of that old piano as it trundled out all the old sentimental, ephemeral tunes ... 'Smoke Gets in Your Eyes', 'Cigarette in the Dark', 'Night and Day' and 'As Time Goes By'. Somehow, whether it was the experience or the smoke, I could not be sure, it almost brought tears to my eyes. I felt conscious of a tremendous wish to stay there forever, never to move from that spot, that moment, that experience.

And yet, of course, in the end I knew that I had to go. Indeed, there was a certain pressure on me in the end, a feeling that I had overstayed my time. By now I had given up trying to find my friends; indeed, they had obviously not come. I stood at the door, taking one last look around, wondering if, perhaps, I might see them.

I shall never forget my last lingering view of the scene, the couples arm-on-arm, singing, the smoky air, the sentimental piano music. How strangely settled they seemed there, as if, indeed, they would never move. For a moment I almost called out to them: 'Is anyone coming? Does anyone want a ride?' But somehow I knew I would call in vain; they would go on and on, singing and laughing, pirouetting in their slow, sad dances. So I shut the doors, went out to my car, and drove off into the now darkened night.

It was around noon the next day before I saw my friends again. I at once accused them of missing a good evening.

They looked at me in amazement. 'Come off it – we couldn't find the place. It's been closed down for years. We asked someone today.'

'Don't be silly,' I said. 'I went there.'

'You're having us on,' one of them laughed.

I don't know why, but I felt quite angry. 'All right, to settle it, I'll drive you there now.'

As it was a fine day, they did not mind. This time we all

went together in a large car. The driver professed to remember the directions, but it was a good thing I was there to guide him. Otherwise, I felt sure, we would never have found the right road. At last we arrived at those massive stone gateways.

'There,' I exclaimed. 'Now you'll see.'

As we turned up the drive, I was puzzled not to see the huge sign, 'The Silver Wings Club'. But there could be no doubting the rhododendron bushes lining the drive, nor the wide sweep up to the huge manor house. As we came round that final bend, the words were on the tip of my tongue: 'There – now do you believe me?'

But they were never uttered. For now, as the big car came gently to a stop, and my friends looked at me in astonishment, I saw in front of me the stone steps and the massive porchway, and the beginnings of old ivy-coloured walls – but nothing else. For the rest of the manor house was a mere shell, a frame – nothing, in fact, except hollow emptiness, green grass growing out of old stone floorways, collapsed stairways leading to nowhere: a gutted memorial.

I don't know how long we sat in the car staring at this – this apparition. I think my friends must have realised that I was really shocked, for they were sympathetic in their gentle questions: 'Is this the place?'

I stared. Yes, this was it, there could be no doubt. But ...?

As if in answer to my unspoken question, we suddenly caught sight of an old man leading a dog across the nearby fields, and called him over.

'Excuse me,' I said, 'but I wonder if you can help me – I thought there was a club here. The Silver Wings Club?'

I felt the old man looking at me curiously.

'The Silver Wings? Ah, yes that's what it used to be – a good many years ago.'

'But – but –?' I stared at the old man, almost appealing. 'What happened?'

The old man leaned on his bike and surveyed the hulk of what had once been the Silver Wings Club. 'T'was during the war – you see, there was a big RAF Station then, just down the road, and them pilots and the WAAFS, they all used to come here every evening. It was their club, you see. Lively lot they were, too. Ah yes.'

He paused for a moment, and I could feel him remembering their gaiety – a gaiety which, somehow, I felt I, too, had witnessed.

'Yes?' I said, unable to wait any longer.

'It was the Germans,' he continued, 'the German bombers. They must have been aiming for the aerodrome, of course. They were coming back from a raid on Plymouth one night. They dropped several fire bombs direct on the club.'

'And were there people there?' I said, my voice almost a whisper. 'Dancing and drinking –?'

'Oh, yes,' said the old man. 'It was very sad, very sad – a whole crowd of them there were. Nearly all killed ...'

The old man went on talking then, about the club, about the gay times there, and about the way things had changed since. But I hardly listened. I was waiting only to ask one more question, and somehow I knew the answer already. 'What was the date when the club was bombed?'

'Why, let me see, it was the first Saturday in July,' said the old man; and then paused, as if surprised. 'Why fancy,' he went on, 'that was last night.'

I felt my friends eyeing me curiously, but suddenly I did not wish to talk about the subject any more. I did not even want to go and walk about the ruins to try and convince myself, either that I had been there, as I imagined, or that I had not. Now there was nothing there, just old ruins. And yet, what if sometimes ruins come to life, we touch some chord, or happen to interrupt an anniversary? Who can possibly say, one way or another, in an age when we are just dimly beginning to understand our massive ignorances?

I only know that some other year, on a certain night in July, I think I shall make that drive again in search of an old manor house, where golden-haired men and women laugh and sing and dance eternally, and a tinkling piano plays those old sweet songs.

XIV

The Top Coat

Peter Tinniswood

The top coat was made of rufous tweed.

It hung from a bruised brass hook at the back of the staff room door.

A quiff of green lining sprouted from the collar top. The rims of the patch pockets were frayed. The buckle on the belt was bent.

I remember it well.

I remember, too, Katz and his *Speisewagen*.

Katz, bald, water-eyed, bow-tied; his *Speisewagen* was his briefcase. It bulged with scraps of food donated by his pupils.

At the top the food was fresh. At the bottom it putrefied.

'A meal from my *Speisewagen*, Herr Brandon,' he would roar, eyes rolling, pale nostrils flickering.

And he would plunge his hands into the depths of his brief case and produce a writhing hulk of putrescent sausage.

Times were hard in Germany when I taught there.

I remember two of my pupils, Fritz and Fraulein Schnee. Fritz with timid lips and plump, placid Fraulein Schnee; it was in a drainage ditch they met their deaths.

I remember Frau Leitner. She was secretary of our school. Her hair was blonde, rucked up fiercely beneath a Tyrolean hat. Her skirts were square. Her feet were firm.

I remember Petitjean, Tom Bailey, Tilly, Frau Grotsch, Professor Smiss, head of English, born Cracow, holder of Portuguese passport, unable to pronounce his 'th's'. I think of them now with pleasure.

I remember the top coat.

I think of it now with terror.

Frau Leitner met me off the train, when I arrived in that sulky German town.

'Herr Brandon?' she said.

'Yes.'

'Herr Hallam Brandon?'

'Correct.'

She shook my hand. She led me to the buffet and ordered coffee.

'You had a good journey from England?' she said.

'I did.'

A film of sadness passed over her pale green eyes. She shook her head softly. Then she smiled.

'You will not like our school, Herr Brandon,' she said.

'Oh?'

'People do not stay for a long time.'

'Why's that?'

She smiled again.

'Drink your coffee and follow me,' she said.

I followed her through cobbled streets. Mattresses drooped over wrought-iron balconies. Hunters from the autumn forests loitered outside gunsmiths. The air was filled with the scents of fresh *Semmeln*.

Frau Leitner stopped outside a thin, whey-faced building with shuttered windows and peeling stucco.

She pointed to a brass plate let into the wall.

It read:

'KRETSCHMER'S PRIVATE ACADEMY FOR THE STUDY OF FOREIGN LANGUAGES.'

She turned and looked up into my eyes. The rufous tints in her pale green eyes flashed.

'This way,' she said, and she led me through a damp courtyard, up two flights of stooping stairs, along a broad corridor to a small hallway.

At the far end stood double glass-fronted doors.

Behind them was Kretschmer's Private Academy.

Frau Leitner led me inside.

'The staff room,' she said, pointing to a door at the end of a narrow passage.

She rested her hand on my forearm. I turned to look down into her pale green eyes. Not a flicker. Her fingers insinuated themselves slowly but insistently into the flesh of my arm. Her firm knee brushed the calf of my leg.

A force I had never felt before flashed through my body. It held me rigid, powerless, taut. Then in an instant it was gone.

'Herr Brandon,' she said very gently. 'Herr Brandon, you will not like it here.'

She turned abruptly and click-clacked away. She did not look back.

I lit a cigarette, walked slowly down the passage and pushed open the door of the staff room.

Tom Bailey looked up and smiled, Petitjean, feet on table, mouth full of cheese and peppers, raised a half-full glass of beer and nodded. Katz rolled his eyes and Frau Grotsch snored peacefully in the corner by the water dispenser.

A gust of wind whipped through the shutters.

Papers flew off the table. The door slammed to behind me.

Very slowly the rufous tweed coat slid to the floor.

I bent down to pick it up.

'For Christ's sake, don't!'

The cry was harsh. Fearful. Prickled by panic.

I spun round.

Tom Bailey's face was white. Petitjean's mouth hung open. Katz's hand trembled. Frau Grotsch sat bolt upright in her chair.

'Never ever touch that coat,' said Tom Bailey, and now there was a hysterical tremble in his voice.

I looked round their faces. There was fear in their eyes.

'Never ever,' said Tom Bailey firmly.

The door opened. Frau Leitner entered. She looked at the faces of my new colleagues. She looked at me. She looked down at the coat. She began to laugh.

It was a hollow laugh with echoes of sadness and bitterness.

It went on and on.

Then she stooped, picked up the coat and hung it once more on the bruised brass hook.

'There,' she said. 'There you are, my poor friends.'

'So come on then, Tom, who owns that bloody coat?'

Tom Bailey glanced across at Petitjean. The Frenchman shrugged his shoulders. The sickle of black moustache glistened with globs of beer.

'For God's sake I've been here two months now, and every time I mention the coat, look at the coat, go anywhere near the bloody coat, everyone just about shits themselves with terror,' I said.

We were sitting in the back room of the inn with the slender chimneys where storks nested in the summer.

It was winter. The weather was bleak. The forests groaned with snow. It was the end of the month. We were broke.

The pot-bellied stove next to the *Stammtisch* rumbled.

So did our stomachs. For three days we had not eaten a hot meal. It would be two days more before we could afford to.

'Well?' I said. 'Who's going to tell me about the coat?'

Tilly sighed.

'All right,' she said.

A tall, straight girl with spikey breasts was Tilly. There were times when she shared Petitjean's bed.

'The coat belonged to Morgan,' she said.

'Morgan?'

'He was a teacher here about three years ago. None of us ...'

'I wish you wouldn't do this,' said Tom Bailey, and his face was anxious and his fingers were agitated.

'Carry on, Tilly,' I said firmly.

She looked at Petitjean. He nodded.

'None of us here knew him,' she said. 'He was before our time. Katz knew him, though. He said he was a loner, rarely spoke, Mostly he was drunk. Not obviously drunk. Privately drunk, you know?

'The strange thing was he never took off his top coat. Even in summer he kept it on. Even when he was teaching. Katz said he kept a silver flask in one of the pockets. He used to drink from it when he thought no one was looking. Katz said it was a milky green liquid. He'd never seen anything like it.'

She paused and drained the last drop of her beer.

Petitjean nodded towards Fritz and Fraulein Schnee who

were holding hands silently in a corner of the room.

Very softly I tapped the bottom of my empty glass on the table.

Fritz jumped up. He came to our table, clicked his heels and bowed his head stiffly.

'*Noch Bier*,' said Petitjean thickly.

'But of course. Most certainly,' said Fritz.

He summoned Ilse from the kitchen where she was dozing with the lean black cat. He ordered more beer. She brought it. He smiled, bowed again and returned to plump, placid Fraulein Schnee.

'Carry on, Tilly,' I said. 'Tell me more.'

Tilly nestled her head on Petitjean's shoulder. He smiled and placed his hand carelessly over her right breast. She sighed.

Then she continued:

'One night — it was about this time of year, too — he got really drunk. Frau Leitner tried to calm him. He ranted and raved. He hit her on the cheek. Then he stormed out.

'No one saw him for three days.

'Then he was found.

'He was in a drainage ditch in the forest.

'He was naked.

'His throat had been cut from ear to ear.'

Tom Bailey began to tremble.

Tilly took a long drink from her beer.

'Four days later a parcel came to the school. Frau Leitner opened it. Inside was the top coat. She didn't say a thing. She just hung it on the back of the staff room door and left.

'Well, there was this Welsh teacher called Rees. He was broke like all of us. He was always cold, too. So one night he took the coat.

'He was never seen again. Four days later the coat was returned. Frau Leitner hung it on the door.

'Then last year the same thing happened to Baldwin.'

'We were all here then,' said Tom Bailey. 'We didn't think anything of it when Katz pleaded with him not to take the coat.'

'We just laughed at him,' said Tilly.

'Baldwin laughed, too,' said Tom Bailey. 'He took the coat one night and said he was off for a pub crawl.'

'We never saw him again,' said Tilly quietly. 'But four days later the coat was returned.'

'Dreadful. Bloody dreadful,' said Tom Bailey.

The stove rumbled.

The lean black cat curled up in front of it. There were specks of rufous in the tip of its tail.

My beer stood untouched on the table. I ran my finger down the icy moisture on the side of the glass.

'So that's why you won't touch it?' I said.

Tom Bailey and Tilly nodded.

'But why Frau Leitner? Why can she touch it?'

Silence.

Tilly and Tom Bailey looked away from me. Petitjean concentrated on stroking Tilly's breast.

I laughed.

'You're pulling my pisser,' I said.

'No,' said Tilly. 'No.'

There was a searing, desperate urgency in her voice. She pulled herself away from Petitjean and took hold of both my hands.

'I mean it, Hallam,' she said. 'Promise me, please, you'll never touch that coat.'

I dipped the tip of my index finger into my glass of beer.

'Please,' she said, gripping my hands tightly. 'Please, Hallam.'

'All right,' I said.

An hour later Tilly left the inn with Petitjean.

She kissed me lightly on the forehead.

Tom Bailey accepted another glass of schnapps off Fritz, drained it in a single gulp and lurched off into the night.

I stood up stiffly and made my way to the corner table, where Fritz cuddled plump, placid Fraulein Schnee.

The schnapps bit hard into the back of my neck and I stumbled against the table.

Fritz jumped up, pulled back a chair for me, bowed and seated me with much decorum.

'*Noch Schnapps, Fritzchen,*' I said.

'But of course. Most certainly,' said Fritz.

Ilse brought schnapps and beer.

I swilled them down.

Ilse brought more schnapps and beer.

Fritz took off his spectacles and rubbed them nervously on the cuff of his jacket.

'Herr Brandon, I have something to tell you,' he said.

'Fire away,' I said.

Fritz blinked rapidly. He coughed. He licked his timid lips. Then he said:

'Tonight Fraulein Schnee and I are to run away from my father.'

I lowered my chin to my chest and looked at him through the tops of my eyes.

I did not speak.

Fritz cleared his throat and took hold of the hand of plump, placid Fraulein Schnee. He looked at me. His eyes were pleading.

'Well?' he said. 'Well?'

A slow smile came to my face.

'Whoopee,' I said very deliberately.

He gave a short sharp laugh.

Whoopee, Fritz, I said to myself. Whoopee, you poor misfortunate German prick.

Pictures of Fritz in the autumn flashed across my mind.

A visit to his home in the heart of the forest. The shriek of saws from his father's mill. Schnapps for breakfast. The stately alpine house with the swooping eaves. Fraulein Schnee tapping softly at the secretary's typewriter in the father's office. Sunday afternoon alone in the house. A cry of pain from along the corridor outside my bedroom. Padding on tip toe along the polished boards. A grunt of pleasure. Peering through half-open bedroom door. Fritz's father naked. Fraulein Schnee, too. Straddling her man, broad back to his face, clenching tight to his stand of timber.

Slowly I stood up from the table.

'Whoopee, you poor misfortunate German prick,' I said.

Outside the cold was cruel.

It ached in my bones.

I shook my head to clear it from the fumes of schnapps. For a moment I felt nausea in my stomach. I reeled against a wall.

Then I saw it.

A light in the window of the school. And in the window the figure of a woman. For the briefest of seconds it stood there outlined, black and sharp. Then it was gone.

My head cleared in an instant.

Rapidly I crossed the street, hurried through the courtyard, ran up the two flights of stairs and flung open the double glass-fronted doors of the school.

Darkness. Silence.

'Hullo,' I shouted. 'Anyone there?'

No answer.

I looked around. A crack of light shone from beneath the door of the staff room.

My heart began to pound. Very carefully I walked along the passage. I paused outside the door. Gingerly my hand approached the handle. Then suddenly I thrust my shoulder against the door and burst it open.

On the floor in front of me lay the rufous ginger top coat.

On the door behind me as I stepped inside hung the Tyrolean hat and skirt of Frau Leitner.

'Frau Leitner,' I screamed. 'Frau Leitner!'

No answer.

A long, slow silence.

I blundered out of the staff room shouting her name.

Wildly, fearfully I looked in classrooms, toilets, the small office she shared with slow, doleful Gudrun, the stockroom with its tattered files and spent staples, the cramped kitchen where Professor Smiss brewed his oxtail soup, the heavy-jowelled office where the Director of the Academy smoked snub yellow cigars and drew pictures of naked ladies on sweaty sheets of pink blotting paper.

'Frau Leitner!' I shouted. 'Frau Leitner!'

No answer.

No sign of life.

Then very slowly and very softly I felt a steady pressure in the skin of my forearm and the calf of my leg.

A force I had felt only two months ago took hold of me.

I fought against it. My voice screamed inside my head. The muscles of my body contorted. Every nerve end shrieked.

Useless.

I found myself back in the staff room.

I found myself bending over the rufous ginger top coat.

I found myself picking it up and rubbing it against my cheeks.

'Frau Leitner,' I sobbed. 'Frau Leitner.'

The force inside me grew stronger. It overwhelmed me.

I found myself outside in the street.

I was wearing the top coat.

I tried to rip it off.

Useless.

I was helpless against the force that pumped through my veins, hammered at my temples, stifled the frightened blubbering voice within my head, suffused the light around me with a shimmering milky green.

The force grew stronger. It turned my head and compelled me to look up at the lighted window of the staff room.

Once more the female figure was outlined there.

'Frau Leitner,' I bellowed.

But no sound came. Not a single word.

I walked through the town with purposeful tread.

The last tram to the depot bucked, bounced and curtsied over the cobbles.

The whores sat motionless and sullen in the windows of the municipal brothel.

A priest vomited in the gutter.

I found myself in a part of the town that was unknown to me.

Yet still I walked on with decisive steps, turning corners

confidently, crossing streets, cutting through a narrow alley rutted with frost-scoured mud and chuttering softly with sleepy fowl.

I walked past stately houses with long brooding gardens, and my footsteps rang out on the cold flags.

I came to a small park. Without hesitation I passed through the gates and strode on steadily past children's swings stark in the moonlight and the frost on the shale tennis court crisscrossed with the footprints of rats.

Unerringly I found a gap in the high laurel hedge and squeezed through.

I was in a garden. Outhouses crouched in the shadows. The grass was unkempt and tangled. On the style of the sundial a blackbird perched frozen in death.

I began to shiver.

For a wild second I felt free to cast off the top coat.

I tore at the buttons. I wrenched at the sleeves.

But then the force deep within me took control again and led me round the side of the house. My feet crunched on gravel. I came to the front portico. I pulled on the bell which hung by the side of the black oak door.

Immediately the door was opened and I stepped inside.

All was in gloom.

I picked out furniture shrouded in white sheets. I heard the clink of glass chandeliers. I smelt dust. I saw before me a broad, double-banked marble staircase.

'This way, *mein Herr*.'

The man stood in the shadows to my right.

I thought I recognized the voice. I hesitated.

'This way, if you please.'

I followed the man as he picked his way through the mounds of furniture.

I recognized the figure.

It was Katz.

'Katz,' I said. 'What the bloody hell are you doing here?'

He did not turn round. I followed him up the marble staircase. He led me along the landing lined with mirrors and prints of Klimt.

He opened a door and nodded.

'In there, *mein Herr*,' he said.

I paused.

'For Christ's sake, what's going on, Katz?' I said.

A voice called from inside the room.

'Please come inside.'

It was the voice of Frau Leitner.

It called again.

'You will like it here. You will find it all most satisfactory, Herr Morgan.'

She was waiting for me when I stepped inside.

Everything was in darkness save for a single shudderingly bright spotlight which picked her out from the blackness.

But it was a Frau Leitner I had never seen before.

No Tyrolean hat, no square skirt, no bulky jumper, no thick woollen stockings.

Her blonde hair tumbled free and unrestrained over naked shoulders. She wore a long crimson gown cut low to show a deep cool cleft between firm noble breasts. The lids of her eyes were painted with kohl of deepest hue, her cheeks were powdered and her lips glistened moistly.

She stepped forward, clasped me round the waist and kissed me long and hard on the lips.

A lance of ice thrust up into my guts. Spikes of ice chattered in the hairs on the nape of my neck.

'Welcome home, Herr Morgan,' she said.

I opened my mouth to scream, but no sound came.

And then suddenly the room was flooded with light.

Snow white walls. Snow white floor. Coal black chairs.

And strapped to each chair by thongs of twisted leather were my friends and colleagues in the town – Tom Bailey, Tilly, Professor Smiss, Frau Grotsch, slow, doleful Gudrun, the Director of our Academy – all with white faces and wide open unblinking eyes frozen with terror as biting as the cold which froze the blackbird on the sundial.

Frau Leitner pressed herself into my body.

'You are shivering, Herr Morgan,' she whispered.

Then she laughed softly and placed her hand into the right

hand pocket of my top coat. She withdrew a silver flask. She took out the stopper. She pressed it to my lips.

'Drink, Herr Morgan,' she said.

I drank some of the milky green liquid.

'More,' she said.

I drained the flask.

I seemed to float as she took me by the arm and led me to the centre of the room.

My whole body was lulled by a gentle, insidious, aching, corrupting, scented warmth as she laid me down on the brocaded divan.

She knelt down beside me.

I felt her breath on my cheek. I felt the touch of her long blonde hair on my neck. I felt the warmth of her body.

'Close your eyes, Herr Morgan,' she said.

My eyes closed. I was powerless to prevent it.

'Look hard, Herr Morgan,' she whispered.

I strained my eyes behind the closed lids.

Darkness. Black. Bruised.

'Harder, harder, Herr Morgan.'

A great roaring filled my ears. My heart thudded. My limbs twitched and then broke down into long juddering spasms.

And then pictures appeared on the insides of the closed lids.

They were clear and sharp in the centre, blurred at the edges in a milky green light.

I saw an attic. In the centre was a bed. On it lay a man in a rufous tweed top coat. He was a broad, bulky man with sleek black hair and a jagged white scar on the bridge of his nose.

I saw the door of the attic open. Into the room stepped Frau Leitner. She tore off her Tyrolean hat and her blonde hair tumbled asunder.

Blackness for a moment. Then another picture.

I saw a path deep in the heart of the forest. It was springy underfoot with needles of pine. I felt their suppleness in the soles of my feet. The path led to a glade. Milky green sunlight filtered down through the canopy of trees. In the centre was spread open a rufous tweed top coat. On it lay the broad, bulky man and Frau Leitner. They fondled gently and kissed.

Blackness. Another picture.

I saw a room with flowered wallpaper, vases of spring flowers, curtains rustling in the breeze, wooden *Schwarzwald* dolls on the pink flounced dressing table.

There was a bed.

On it lay Frau Leitner. She wore a nightgown of whitest silk unbuttoned to the waist. Her nipples glowed brown beneath the silk.

The door opened. In stepped the broad bulky man in the rufous tweed top coat. He tore it off. And then the milky green light clouded my vision and I heard sobs and slow groans and sighs and a long piercing cry.

Blackness.

This time the picture was dazzling and clear.

I saw a bedroom in an alpine house with swooping eaves. I heard the whine of saws. Naked on the bed were the broad, bulky man and Frau Leitner. She straddled him. Her wide back was turned to his contorted, perspiring face.

Her breasts swung free.

In her hand she held a long thin curved knife.

The door opened.

In stepped Fritz and plump, placid Fraulein Schnee.

Frau Leitner looked up and screamed. And screamed and screamed.

I opened my eyes as her hand bit deep into the flesh of my cheek.

The room was in darkness once more save for the single spotlight which bore down on the divan where I lay.

Frau Leitner's tongue searched the rim of my ear.

Her hands curved down my thighs.

'And now, Herr Morgan, it is time to look,' she said presently.

She put her hand behind my neck and raised my head from the arm of the divan.

In front of me she held a hand mirror.

'Look,' she said.

I looked into the mirror.

It was not my face I saw.

I saw the face of a broad, bulky man with sleek black hair and jagged white scar across the bridge of his nose.

And out of his neck from ear to ear a slow, steady stream of blood oozed down on to his chest.

I screamed.

Loud and long.

And this time the sound came tumbling, flooding, cascading from deep within my soul.

It was just after dawn when the police came to my room.

They led me outside to their car.

They drove me to the forest.

They led me to a drainage ditch.

Over it was a canopy of plastic.

They pulled it back.

In the ditch lay two bodies.

'Well?'

I nodded.

'Yes,' I said. 'Those are my pupils, Fritz and Fraulein Schnee.'

The cold ached in my bones.

But I could not move.

I could not tear my eyes away from the body of Fritz.

It was wrapped in the rufous tweed top coat.

Four days later I left the school.

Frau Leitner escorted me to the station.

When the train drew into the platform, she took hold of my hand and gripped it firmly.

'Goodbye, Herr Brandon,' she said.

Then she clasped me around the waist and kissed me long and hard on the lips.

'I am sorry you do not wish to stay,' she whispered. 'There were so many things we could have done together.'

I leaned out of the carriage window and held her hand.

The steam rose around her legs.

Whistles blew.

She bent and took something out of her canvas bag.

'For you,' she said, and then she blew a kiss as the train drew away.

I watched her until the train curved away from the station.

She did not move for a while.

Then quickly she tore off her Tyrolean hat, and her long, lustrous, silky blonde hair streamed out behind her in the crisp winter air.

The train gathered speed.

The forest flashed by.

I looked at the bulky parcel she had taken from her bag.

And then with all my might I hurled it out of the window.

Zoë Meadows.
24 December 1984.

£2.50.